A Susceptible
Gentleman

A Susceptible
Gentleman

Carola Dunn

Five Star • Waterville, Maine

Published in 2004 in conjunction with Carola Dunn.

The text of this edition is unabridged.

Set in 11 pt. Plantin by Elena Picard.

Printed in the United States on permanent paper.

Library of Congress Cataloging-in-Publication Data

Dunn, Carola.
    A susceptible gentleman / Carola Dunn.
      p. cm.
    ISBN 1-59414-264-5 (hc : alk. paper)
      1. Clergy — Family relationships — Fiction.
  2. Mistresses — Fiction. 3. Villages — Fiction.
  4. England — Fiction. I. Title.
PR6054.U537S87 2004
823′.914—dc22   2004056296

A Susceptible Gentleman

Chapter One

<+- +>

"We must buy some more ginger," said Sarah Meade, weighing the last of the reddish-yellow powder on the little brass scales. "There is just enough. And we are running out of currants for the eyes. I have chopped the candied peel and stolen a glass of brandy from Jonathan's keg. Is the sugar dissolved yet, Mrs. Hicks?"

The plump cook-housekeeper turned from the carrots she was dicing for that night's dinner to stir the mixture of butter and sugar melting in a saucepan on the stove.

"Aye, Miss Sarah, 'tes ready. Did you measure out the treacle?"

"Yes, and a messy job it is. Still, everything is much easier since Jonathan bought the closed stove, and the Sunday school children do love gingerbread men."

"Half on 'em wouldn't show up, else," said Mrs. Hicks cynically. "Hark, now, summun's scratching at the back door. If 'tes one o' they gypsies I'll give un a piece o' me mind." She bustled through the scullery to open the door. "Why, if it bain't Nan Wootton. Never see hide nor hair of you in church but 'tes the vicarage you run to when there's trouble. What's up, then, girl?"

"Be Miss Meade at home?" came a doleful voice, punctuated by a sniff.

"What is it, Nan?" called Sarah, brushing back with

7

floury fingers the curly wisps of dark hair that always escaped the severe coiffure she considered suitable for a vicar's sister. "Come into the kitchen, my dear, and tell me what I can do for you."

The girl who scurried in, followed by a disapproving Mrs. Hicks, was a sorry sight. Her pretty, round-cheeked face was disfigured by a black eye, her ash-blonde hair dishevelled, and her apron torn and muddy round the hem. Upon seeing Sarah, she burst into tears.

"Oh, miss!" she wailed.

Sarah gently urged her to sit down and explain her troubles. Drawn by the commotion, the Meades' housemaid, Nellie, stuck her head into the room.

"I'll wager I can guess what's up wi' that one," she observed. "No better than she should be, she ain't."

Mrs. Hicks shooed her out and tactfully went after her, closing the door.

"Oh, miss," sobbed Nan, "I got a bun in the oven and me Da hit me and me Mam throwed me out o' the house."

Sarah patted her shoulder comfortingly. "Who is the father?" she asked. Though Jonathan's parishioners were in general a well-behaved lot, this was by no means an unknown occurrence in the village of Little Fittleton.

"Might be Jem, as is ostler over to the George at Amesbury. He won't have nothing to do wi' me no more."

Sarah sighed. When there was more than one possible father, the outcome was rarely a wedding.

"Or might be Corporal Ritchie. He were quartered at Bulford, miss, and he told me he'd marry me and take me to London, and now the regiment's gone and what am I to do?"

"I must talk to Mr. and Mrs. Wootton. I'm sure they will take you back, Nan."

"Da said he niver wants to set eyes on me agin. I'm afeard to go home, miss, honest."

"Then there's no help for it. I shall send you to Lord Cheverell's home."

"Oh, miss, 'is lordship won't want the likes o' me."

"His lordship has founded a home for unwed mothers," Sarah explained, hiding a smile, though she knew she should be shocked at the girl's assumption. "It is in Kensington, near London. I shall give you the address and buy you a ticket on the stage and you will need a pound or two for other expenses. They will take care of you there, I promise you, and the baby when it comes." She opened the kitchen door and called, "Mrs. Hicks! Pray take Nan upstairs to tidy herself. I must go and tell Arthur to put Dapple to the gig to take her to Amesbury to catch the London stage. He can buy ginger and currants while he is there, and see if you can think of anything else we need."

Within half an hour Nan, tearful and apprehensive, was driven off by the grumpy manservant. Sarah returned to her gingerbread men. As she stirred the flour into the congealed mixture of treacle, butter and sugar, her thoughts were not with the errant farm girl but with Adam Lancing, Viscount Cheverell.

Growing up at nearby Cheve House with a choleric father, an adoring mother, and four worshipful younger sisters, Adam had developed a strong empathy for female suffering. Since inheriting the title and the huge fortune that went with it, he had founded not only the home for unwed mothers but three orphanages for destitute girls and an almshouse for elderly gentlewomen. Sarah knew he took a personal interest in the management of these refuges, and in the welfare of their residents. In fact, he often consulted both Jonathan and herself on how to improve conditions and on the problems of individuals in his care.

The Meades had known Adam forever. Their father had been vicar of Little Fittleton, appointed by the late viscount as Jonathan had been appointed by the present holder of the title. Adam and Jonathan were the same age, seven and twenty now, and had been as close as brothers since early childhood.

Sarah, three years younger, had followed them into scrapes and adventures with a dogged persistence that had sometimes earned her snubs, sometimes grudging acceptance and occasionally admiration. She had scorned to sit with Adam's sisters sewing her sampler.

She had also shared the boys' lessons with the Reverend Meade until they had been sent off to Eton. At that point her mother had taken over her education. To such effect did Mrs. Meade inculcate the domestic virtues that upon her death, when Sarah was eighteen, the vicarage continued to run as smoothly as ever. Indeed, there were those who thought that the scholarly and absentminded vicar had scarcely noticed his wife's absence before he joined her not a year later in the graveyard of his own church.

For six years now Sarah had kept house for her brother, comforted his flock, helped him write his sermons, and taught the village children Bible stories in Sunday school. She had had her share of admirers, and more than one proposal of marriage. None had tempted her to leave Jonathan.

Only one man could ever do that, she thought wistfully as she rolled the sticky dough and started cutting out the gingerbread figures. But he regarded her as a friend, almost a sister. There had never been anything in the least romantic in the way Adam Lancing looked at Sarah Meade.

She sighed.

"Lawks, Miss Sarah, you've gone and put three eyes and

two noses on that one," exclaimed Mrs. Hicks. "Not worryin' yer head 'bout that hussy, I hope."

Sarah picked off the extra currants and absently ate them.

"No, she will do very well at Lord Cheverell's home," she said.

At that moment her brother wandered in. Though Sarah was tall, the Reverend Jonathan Meade topped her by a head. They were both slim, with dark brown hair and the same grey eyes flecked with gold. A handsome pair, was the general consensus. Nor did those who held the motto Handsome is as Handsome Does, find anything to cavil at. The vicar of Little Fittleton and his sister were welcome in the houses of rich and poor, noble and commoner alike.

"Whom have you sent to Adam's home?" Jonathan enquired, stealing a scrap of dough. "Delicious," he added in a muffled voice.

"Poor Nan Wootton. Don't take any more or there will not be enough to go around. She does not know who is the father, I fear, and Farmer Wootton has disowned her."

"I'll have a talk with him. Sometimes I wonder whether anyone hears a word I say about Christian charity."

"At least you do not need to preach to Adam on that subject. His concern for the unfortunate is beyond praise."

"Yes, on *that* subject there is nothing to be said," Jonathan agreed, with a dry inflexion that his sister missed.

"I daresay he will be here shortly. Jane has quarrelled with Lord Bradfield again and run home to Cheve, and Lady Cheverell told me she has sent for Adam to sort them out."

"Jane is a silly young woman," the vicar said with unwonted severity, "as are all the Lancing girls. Not a ha'p'orth of sense between them. Not one of them can hold a candle to you, my dear."

"Thank you, kind sir." Sarah dimpled and curtsied. "Mrs. Hicks, open the oven, if you please. Here are Shadrach, Meshach and Abednego, and friends, ready to enter the burning fiery furnace."

"When Adam comes, do you mean to ask him about supporting your school?" asked Jonathan, nabbing another pinch of dough while Sarah's back was turned.

"Yes. Do you think he will? So many people seem to think it foolish, even wrong, to teach common children to read and write, especially girls."

"Adam has always respected your judgement."

Sarah hoped the heat of the oven would explain her pink cheeks.

"I seem to remember a certain occasion when he had to carry me down from the top of a larch tree . . ."

He grinned. "Never let you forget that, did he? Don't worry, I expect he will give you the funds to set up your school. I must go and start on Sunday's sermon. Bring me Shadrach when he is baked, will you? Payment for the brandy you put in the dough."

An hour later, Sarah left her brother nibbling on a gingerbread man in his study and returned to the kitchen to wrap several more in a clean linen napkin.

"Johnny Cratch hurt his leg and won't be able to come to Sunday school," she explained to Mrs. Hicks as she put them in a basket. "And little Mary Sopwith is feverish, and Esmeralda Buddle has the earache."

"Won't be none left come Sunday," grumbled Mrs. Hicks as her mistress set off with the basket on her arm. "Too kind-'earted by arf."

Chapter Two

"Why, I do believe I am almost jealous of your husband!" said Lord Cheverell, grinning at his mistress as he shrugged his broad shoulders into his evening coat of midnight-blue superfine. Though elegantly cut, it was loose enough to allow of dispensing with the services of his valet. Lord Cheverell rarely spent a night within reach of his valet.

"I adore you, Adam," Janet Goudge assured him, "but you know I am monstrous fond of Henry. His ship should reach London tomorrow, so I shall not be able to see you again."

The dawn light creeping round the richly brocaded curtains was kind to Mrs. Goudge, who could give Adam three or four years. Dark and voluptuous, she curled around him when he sat on the edge of the bed to pull on his boots.

"You are not angry, are you?" she coaxed.

He patted her shoulder and kissed her cheek in a brotherly fashion. "Of course not, my pet. It was my pleasure to console you in your loneliness."

"I *was* lonely. Henry has been in India for almost two years. I am sure his fortune is quite large enough to make it unnecessary to go again."

"That reminds me." Adam stood up and reached into his coat pocket, withdrawing a small package. The India merchant's wife had no need of costly baubles, but it was only gentlemanly to provide a farewell gift, even though it was she who was giving him his congé.

The chiefest charm of Adam Lancing, Viscount Cheverell, was his ability to convince any female in his company that she was loved and protected and important to him.

Not that that was by any means his lordship's only charm. Broad shoulders tapered to narrow hips, and the current fashion for skintight pantaloons suited his muscular legs to perfection. His features were, perhaps, not out of the ordinary, with the exception of a pair of lively, speaking blue eyes. But few feminine fingers had ever been able to resist the urge to brush back from his forehead the vagrant lock of corn-gold hair that invariably escaped the ministrations of his valet.

This Janet promptly did as he leaned down for one final kiss. Before he reached the door the curl had resumed its customary place.

Walking home through the London dawn, Adam felt an unexpected wave of relief. Fond as he was of Janet, it would be pleasant to spend one night in three in his own bed. An alarming thought jolted him: was he growing too old, at twenty-seven, to keep three mistresses happy? Yet it was a sense not of excess but of something missing that assailed him as he entered his Mount Street mansion.

Gammon! Tonight he would be with Marguerite, his flamboyant opera singer; tomorrow, shy, grateful Peggy awaited him in her little Chelsea villa. The world was full of delightful females and he was ever ready to appreciate their charms.

In fact, Adam found most females irresistible. If he had not yet been snaffled by any matchmaking mama, it was because he treated all their hopeful daughters, pretty or plain,

with equal charm, courtesy and kindness. To their peren-
nial despair, they could never discern the slightest indica-
tion of any distinguishing attachment.

After a few hours' sleep and a hearty breakfast, Adam
called at his clubs: White's, because his father had been a
fervent Tory; and Brooks's, because he himself was a fervent, even Radical, Whig. At the former he was joined by
Lord James Kerridge, at the latter by Mr. Frederick
Swanson, two of his particular cronies. Together, the three
friends went on to Tattersall's to see what sort of horseflesh
was for sale that day, and then to Gentleman Jackson's for a
round or two of boxing. Then Adam left his companions
strolling down Bond Street, and made his way to Westminster.

The Parliamentary year was drawing to a close, and with
the festivities attendant upon the arrival of the Allied Mon-
archs in London, little of import was taking place in the
House of Lords. The Marquis of Lansdowne, himself a re-
former, had used his influence to permit young Lord
Cheverell to speak upon his favorite subject.

Adam's attempt to arouse the interest of a few somnolent peers in providing assistance to destitute women was
not a success. In fact, he would have considered it a triumph to awaken some of them at all, since they appeared to
have retreated to Westminster in search of a peaceful place
to sleep. Seething with frustration, he drove home to
change for dinner and an evening at the theatre.

His butler greeted him stiffly, radiating disapproval.

"A young person called, my lord. She refused to leave
without seeing your lordship. I put her in the back parlour."

"Thank you, Gossett." Adam frowned. "I suppose I had
best see her at once. Did she give no name?"

"No, my lord. Shortly thereafter, my lord, another young person called."

Adam groaned.

"In the morning room, my lord. And a third caller, a Mrs. Goudge, she claims, awaits you in the library, my lord. Were you expecting any further visitors, my lord?"

"What the devil has brought them all here!" exclaimed Adam, a rhetorical question ignored by the butler. "I trust they have not seen each other?"

"No, my lord."

Adam braced his shoulders. "First come, first served," he said. "The back parlour it is, Gossett."

In the back parlour, a small, uncomfortable room intended to discourage unwanted visitors, he found Peggy. A pretty, sturdy girl of seventeen or eighteen, dressed in a simple gown of blue muslin, she was huddled in a chair, her eyes red with weeping.

"Adam!" she cried, throwing herself into his arms. "It's Billy!"

With soothing murmurs he led her to a sofa and sat her down.

"Tell me everything, my pet," he urged.

"He's groom up at t'Hall, where I were housemaid. He wanted to wed me, but I come to London instead. He got worried an' come to look for me. Oh Adam, summun told him 'bout you an' me, an' he wants to kill you! I told him and told him how you saved me from that bawdy house where they beat me, but he won't listen. Billy always were that pigheaded," she added with a note of pride.

Adam felt sure there must be a solution, but half his mind was wondering what Janet and his other visitor—Marguerite he assumed—wanted with him.

"I must think," he said in a harried voice. "Wait here a

16

minute, there's a good girl. I'll be right back." He patted her cheek and hurried out.

Marguerite was pacing up and down the morning room, red hair in disarray, eyes flashing, magnificent bosom heaving. Her spangled gown of daffodil satin swirled about her dainty ankles.

"Adam, darling!" Her angry march became a languorous glide. She wound her arms about his neck and kissed him before she went on in a seductive coo with undertones of fury. "That wretched Morris has given Clorinda my part! He promised I should have the lead in the farce. She croaks like a frog but she warms his bed and I am faithful to you, so I end up in the second line of the chorus while she parades centre stage."

"I'll see what I can do, my pet," promised Adam. He had a thousand times rather buy her a diamond necklace than negotiate with her obsequious manager, who had probably already been paid off by Clorinda's protector. "We'll discuss it in a moment. There is something I must do first."

Janet was standing by the library window, gazing out. She was clad from head to toe in black, and when she turned and put back the black veil of her hat her face was pale.

"Adam!" She stepped towards him with both hands held out. "I apologize for coming here, but I have just received word that Henry's ship is sunk and I do not know what to do."

He took her hands and gave them a reassuring squeeze. "Lawyers," he said a trifle wildly. "Relatives. There must be relatives. And business partners. Don't worry, my pet, I shall find people to take care of everything until you recover from the shock."

At that moment, a commotion erupted in the hall.

"You can't come in here, my girl," protested Gossett loudly and angrily.

"Miss Meade said as I were to go to Lord Cheverell's home!" shrilled a female voice. "She give me money to get here. I bain't a-goin' to budge till I seen his lordship. He'll take care o' me, she said."

Adam shuddered. He would do a great deal for Sarah Meade, but this was not the best moment to send him yet another damsel in distress. He strode into the hall.

Janet Goudge followed him, while Marguerite and Peggy emerged from their respective retreats. They stared at each other in astonished horror.

A girl with a black eye and a bulging waistline broke away from the butler, flung herself at his feet and clasped his knees.

"Don't let him throw me out, your worship," she begged. "I come all the way from Little Fittleton on the stage. Miss Meade said as you'd let me stay at your home till the baby comes. Do all them ladies have a bun in the oven, too?" Nan Wootton gazed interestedly at Adam's harem.

Peggy burst into floods of tears.

Janet cast a burning glance of reproach at Adam and said stiffly, "I am a married woman."

Marguerite abandoned her refined accent and poured a torrent of Cockney abuse on his lordship's head.

"Shall I call a pair of footmen to see these, ahem, ladies out, my lord?" enquired Gossett stolidly.

"Yes! No! Dammit, I don't know." Adam looked round in despair. His eyes fell on Nan Wootton. "You should be at the Kensington place, my girl," he said, clutching at a straw. "I'll take you there right away."

The butler coughed meaningfully. "If I might make so bold, my lord," he said, "there's a letter from her ladyship arrived by the second post that your lordship might care to read before leaving." He picked up a silver salver from the hall table and presented it.

"From my mother? Yes, I'd best read it at once." Adam seized the letter and escaped into the library. It was brief and to the point: Adam must come down to Cheve *immediately* to rescue his sister Jane from her folly.

When he reluctantly returned to the hall, scarce two minutes later, it was empty but for Gossett.

"I ventured to inform the, ahem, ladies that you would be in touch as soon as possible, my lord," he said blandly. "The girl awaits your lordship in the kitchen."

Adam suppressed an impulse to hug the butler.

"Gossett, you are a miracle-worker," he said with fervour. "Have my curricle sent round and tell Wrigley to pack up enough for a week at Cheve. He need not come. I'll drop the girl in Kensington and spend the night at the Barley Mow in Englefield Green. If the, ahem, ladies call again, tell them that I am out of town for a few days."

"Yes, my lord," said Gossett.

Driving out of Andover the next afternoon Adam felt his spirits rising. It was a perfect June day; the sky was a cloudless blue arching over the bare green hills of Salisbury Plain. Lost in the blue a lark sang so loudly he heard it clearly over the pounding of his horses' hooves.

He would go first to the vicarage, he decided, to tease Sarah about sending Nan Wootton to him. She would be the person to help him with poor little Peggy, too. How she and Jonathan would laugh at his predicament with the four, ahem, ladies all arriving at the same moment, but they would then give him the benefit of their advice.

He turned off the toll road onto a chalky lane, little more than a track, leading up into the hills. Sheep wandered freely here, nibbling at the short, wiry grass. Adam loved the wide open reaches where the winds blew free and you felt you could see forever. He wondered why he did not spend more time here, instead of in the crowded, smoky city.

Suddenly a pair of sheep decided to dash across the road right under the noses of his team.

The horses shied, snorting in alarm, but the viscount was a top sawyer, a member of the Four-Horse Club, and had them under control in a moment.

"Bravo!"

He looked round at the sound of applause. Sarah Meade rose from her seat on the dry ground and limped towards him.

"Well done, Adam. I thought they would bolt with you."

He grinned, but said with quick anxiety, "Have you hurt yourself? I cannot get down to help you."

"It is merely a broken sandal strap, but I am very glad you came along. How like you to travel without even a groom to display your consequence!"

"And how like you to walk for miles without even a maid to ensure your safety." He leaned down and reached out a hand to help her climb into the curricle, then gave the horses the office to start.

"Lest I should be attacked by wild sheep?" Sarah settled on the leather seat and straightened her straw bonnet. "I went to Stonehenge. It is a marvellous place to sit and think on a day like this, but you know the local people are too superstitious to go near it."

"You cannot gammon me that you ever take a servant

when you go out. By the way, your Nan Wootton is safely installed at Kensington."

Her eyes widened at this, and for the first time in all the years he had known her, he noticed the gold flecks in the grey irises.

"How do you know of that already?" she asked in surprise. "I cannot believe that they inform you at once of each new arrival?"

"No, no, m'dear, I do not keep so close a watch on my protégées. The girl arrived on my doorstep in Mount Street and announced that you had sent her to Lord Cheverell's home."

"Oh Adam, I hope she did not embarrass you!" Her voice was apologetic but the gold flecks seemed to dance with amusement. "Never say you were entertaining guests."

It was the perfect opening for bringing up the problems of Peggy, Marguerite and Janet. He found he had changed his mind. Somehow he no longer wanted to tell Sarah that his three mistresses had all been there when Nan Wootton appeared; Jonathan's counsel must suffice.

"Not entertaining, precisely," he hedged, "but I wish you might have seen my butler's face when she fell to her knees and embraced mine."

Sarah laughed. "Oh dear, the silly child must have lost the address I gave her. She cannot read, you know. And that reminds me of something I want to speak to you about. What is your opinion of education for women?"

"Since you are the best-educated woman I know, I hardly dare venture to say."

"Cut line, Adam! I want to start a school for the village and farm children, especially the girls. Unfortunately, Lady Cheverell believes that teaching the lower classes to read and write will give them ideas above their station."

"You may safely leave Mama to me, m'dear, and my purse is at your disposal."

"Jonathan said I might rely on you. You truly are a 'verray parfit gentil knight.' " Her glowing look of admiration and gratitude disconcerted him.

"I trust you do not mean to teach them Chaucer," he said dryly.

"Heavens, no. They must learn modern English before they can tackle Shakespeare, let alone fourteenth-century literature. To tell the truth, I do not find it easy myself, and I take leave to doubt that you have ever read more than the odd quotation in a book of extracts."

"Alas, I am found out." To Adam's relief, the conversation had recovered its bantering tone. Sarah was the only woman he ever joked with, he realized. He could not bear the thought of losing her regard.

Chapter Three

<+- +>

" 'How happy I could be with either, were t'other dear charmer away!' " the vicar mockingly borrowed from *The Beggar's Opera*.

"Don't you start quoting at me, too," pleaded the viscount. "Besides, it's inaccurate. I was perfectly happy with all three, until they met one another."

"Three was enough, was it?"

"It's all very well for you to roast me, Jon. You're a clergyman, it's different for you."

"Not very," his friend said wryly, tipping his chair back and putting his feet on his desk in a most unclerical posture. "One learns to do without."

"Well I don't believe you have Romish tendencies. Why don't you marry?"

"If Sarah were to wed, I daresay I should seriously look about me for a wife, but I doubt I shall ever meet a woman who measures up to my sister."

"No," said Adam, suddenly thoughtful, "I can see that."

"She has had suitors a-plenty, you know. I'm glad she refused them all, for none was worthy of her. Of course I should not stand in her way if she formed a tendre for some respectable gentleman, however unworthy I thought him."

The viscount was oddly displeased by the idea of Sarah falling in love and marrying. He had spent little time in

Wiltshire these past few years and had not been aware that she had had suitors.

He caught sight of her through the study's French windows, which stood open to the garden. She was talking to Arthur, gardener, groom, and general factotum, as she bent gracefully over a rosebush to cut a perfect yellow bloom. Her dark hair, uncovered, shone in the sun, and though slender her figure was womanly. She was no longer Adam's childhood playmate; in fact many would consider her, at twenty-four, to be nearly on the shelf.

He dismissed the notion with a shrug.

"Of course you will not try to interfere," he agreed shortly. "But tell me, what am I to do with my three charmers?"

"I shall think about it, but you had best consult Sarah," suggested Jonathan. "She is bound to understand females better than you or I."

"Dammit, these are lightskirts, Jon, not respectable tabbies from your congregation!"

"She won't be shocked. She is used to dealing with the likes of Nan Wootton, remember."

Adam shook his head gloomily. He did not expect Sarah to be shocked by Marguerite, Peggy and Janet so much as by his own behaviour. Still, he could hardly tell Jonathan that he did not want to spoil her image of him as a "verray parfit gentil knight."

He resigned himself. "If you say so."

Jonathan let his chair fall with a thump to the well-polished floorboards. He went to the French windows and called.

"Sarah! If you are not too busy, Adam is in sore need of your advice."

She looked up with a smile, waved to him, and said something to Arthur before turning toward the house. Half a dozen roses were gingerly clasped in one hand as she raised the hem of her lavender muslin round gown to mount the terrace steps.

"Ouch!" she exclaimed, entering the study. "I forgot my flower basket. I must put these in a vase; I shall be with you in a minute, Adam."

Afraid that he might turn tail if forced to wait, he objected.

"They will keep," he said, taking the bouquet from her and dropping it on the desk. "Ouch! Are there no thornless flowers as beautiful as roses?"

"No," she told him, annoyed. "And they will wilt if I do not put them in water at once."

"I'll take them to the kitchen," offered her brother pacifically. "I've heard Adam's story already, but I'll be back to discuss solutions."

They heard his "Ouch!" as he closed the study door behind him. Their eyes met and they laughed.

"What is the trouble?" Sarah asked, taking a seat. Adam perched on the corner of the desk. She thought he looked distinctly uneasy.

"I'm sure between us we shall see a way out," she said to encourage him. "Is it something to do with Nan? Or your sister Jane?"

"With Nan, in a way. She really did turn up at a very awkward moment. No, it was not your fault she came to Mount Street! You must not think I blame you in the slightest."

Sarah swallowed her renewed apology and watched with interest as the viscount began to pace restlessly from end to end of the small room.

"You see, there were three, ahem, ladies already in the house."

"Ahem, ladies?" wondered Sarah, eyebrows raised.

Adam hurried on. "They had all come to me for help, but they were unaware of each other's presence. When Nan arrived they all met in the hall and there was something of an explosion. That's beside the point, though. I'd like you to suggest how I can help them with the problems they had come to see me about."

Intrigued, she nodded. "Tell me. Only do for heaven's sake sit down, Adam. I shall go mad if you step on that squeaky board one more time."

He dropped into a chair and ran his fingers through his hair. The vagrant lock flopped back over his brow.

"Well there's Ja—Mrs. Goudge. Her husband is a cit, an India nabob, rich enough to buy an abbey. He's been in the East for the past couple of years and she expected him back any day. Then she heard that his ship was sunk."

"Poor woman! She must be altogether overset. But I do not quite see why she came to you. Perhaps you have business dealings with Mr. Goudge?"

Though Adam was sitting with his back to the window, Sarah saw a slight flush redden his cheeks. She was amused by his embarrassment at being suspected of engaging in trade with a cit. She came to his rescue.

"I daresay she ought to see his lawyer first. Is it certain that the ship was sunk? And that he was on it? Perhaps you ought to enquire further."

"That is an excellent idea!" He seized on her words. "It may be all a hum. Your advice is always good, Sarah."

"But you will need to return to London to assist Mrs. Goudge," she pointed out. "What of the others?"

"Others? Oh, yes, well . . . There's Marguerite. She is a singer. The theatre manager promised her the part of the heroine in a new opera, and then gave it to someone else."

"An opera singer? Why should she suppose that you could do anything for her?" Sarah bit her lip as unwelcome suspicions flitted through her mind. "And why should *you* suppose that *I* know anything of actresses and theatres?"

Adam seemed to be struggling to find an acceptable explanation. He gave up.

"You are quite right, m'dear, it was chuckleheaded of me to expect it. I have come to rely too much upon you and Jonathan."

Sarah, sitting bolt upright with her chin raised, fixed him with a steely eye.

"And what of the third, ahem, lady?" she enquired in a determined voice.

"I scarcely think . . ."

"Tell me, Adam!"

The look he gave her was cool, assessing. She reminded herself that she had no right to judge him, that as well as a friend he was a wealthy young nobleman. And wealthy young noblemen kept mistresses. She had thought him different; she was wrong.

"Perhaps I can help her," she said quietly.

"It's a common story. Peggy is a country girl who went to London to make her fortune. As happens more often than not, she fell into bad company, and no, Sarah, I do not refer to myself. The carriers' carts are met by charming elderly ladies who offer their assistance to the bewildered innocents while they are seeking a position. The only position they find is in a locked room in a brothel, until they resign themselves to the life. Peggy did not resign herself. She ran away. I came across her crouched in a back alley near Seven Dials with the abbess standing over her wielding a horsewhip."

Sarah winced at the image he evoked, but said nothing.

His hard voice softened.

"Yes, I took her under my protection. Yes, she has been my . . . what euphemism do you prefer? . . . my chère amie, shall we say. What other future was there for her? She is a grateful girl, and considers me something of a hero," he added wryly. "But now her country sweetheart has discovered her whereabouts and *he* is after my blood!"

"And you, of course, are terrified!" Sarah attempted a rallying tone. "After the tales Jonathan has told me about your prowess at Manton's Shooting Gallery and Gentleman Jackson's Boxing Saloon! I daresay you can defend yourself, Adam, while I think what is best to be done with your Peggy."

He rose to his feet and took both her hands in his.

"Thank you. I was right to count on you. And now I must be off to Cheve House to see what Jane and my mother have cooked up between them to keep me busy. May I call tomorrow?"

"I shall try to have a suggestion for you by then."

She disengaged her hands and stood up, avoiding his eyes. In the narrow front hall they found Jonathan chatting with Miss Barnes, an elderly parishioner. The viscount paused to greet the sharp-faced old maid, bowing over her hand, and as Sarah escaped up the stair she heard her fluttering response to his easy charm.

She was furious, whether more with herself or with Adam she did not know. What a peagoose she had been to suppose that he was untouched by the common dissipations of his sex and class. She had seen only his friendliness, his kindness to those in need, his lack of arrogance. Not for a moment had she guessed at the rakish disposition hidden beneath, and surely a man who kept three mistresses at once might be called a rake.

She went into her chamber, a small, sunny room that faced the ancient stone church. Kicking off her shoes, she curled up in a shabby but comfortable chair by the window. Adam was a whited sepulcher, she mused, gazing out at the tombstones in the churchyard, fair without and tainted within. Her ready sense of humour came to the fore and she giggled at the thought. Besides, it was not quite just. His good works were not to be despised only because he was not a pattern-card of perfection. Nor must she allow her disillusionment to interfere with accepting his aid for her school.

A delicious aroma of frying onions wafted up from the kitchen below, and Sarah decided to go and see whether Mrs. Hicks needed any help with dinner. Though Nellie was good at dusting and polishing, somehow whenever she entered the kitchen something broke or burned.

Her mind on domestic matters, Sarah started when Jonathan called to her as she passed the study door.

"Have you a moment to spare, my dear?" he asked with his habitual courtesy.

"I daresay Mrs. Hicks will manage without me. What is it?"

The vicar tugged at his clerical collar as if it were suddenly too tight.

"I . . . ah," he began hesitantly, "I wondered whether you had any suggestions for Adam. I was not able to talk to him because of Miss Barnes."

Hands on hips, his sister looked at him with dawning comprehension.

"I believe you did it on purpose," she accused.

"I? On purpose? What?" he enquired in apparent bewilderment, but his cheeks were pink and he did not meet her eyes.

"Jonathan, you did! Adam would never have told me that farrago had you not urged him to it. But why?"

"Do stop towering over me like an avenging fury," he begged. "Sit down. Yes, I did persuade Adam to tell you about his lady friends."

"Have I misunderstood?" She sank into a chair. "Are they not his bits of muslin?"

"Wherever did you learn such a vulgar phrase, Sarah!" The vicar took the offensive.

She blushed, but persisted. "Are they?"

"I'm afraid you are right; they are."

"I believe you have known forever that he had mistresses in keeping! You were not surprised in the least. And now I recall that you hinted he had need of sermons on subjects other than charity. Only I still do not see why you had him tell me."

"I daresay I have been blind," he said ruefully. "For some reason everything came together in my mind today. Just yesterday, talking of Nan Wootton and your school and Adam's charities, I was struck by your excessively high opinion of him. You thought him a paragon, and no man can aspire to perfection. I knew you were bound to be disillusioned sooner or later. And then, today, when he drove you home—my dear, your happy face and the way you looked at him . . . I was afraid you had fallen in love with him. He is the best of friends to us both, but he is also a member of the aristocracy, with his position to consider. Nor do I think he has the least interest in marriage, even to one of his own class."

"Marriage!" Sarah rose to her feet, her dignity marred by the martial light in her eye. "I would not marry Lord Cheverell if he were the last man on earth!"

Chapter Four

The village of Little Fittleton, with its thatched flint-and-stone cottages, lay somnolent under the noonday sun as Adam drove down its single street. The few people he passed smiled as they curtsied or doffed their caps to their landlord. Though rarely at home, he had a good bailiff, and any problems reported to him received his prompt attention. Besides, who could resist the dashing young lord who had run wild about the neighbourhood as a boy and still spoke in the friendliest way to the least of his tenants?

Adam noted with satisfaction that the barley stood tall in the fields, the hairy heads already beginning to bend. A good harvest meant work for all. Most of his wealth came from the sheep on the hills, which offered little employment except at shearing time, but it was a small village and with the Meades to guide him, he made sure no one suffered for lack of work.

He breathed deep of the fresh, clean air and wondered again why he spent so much time in town.

He topped a rise and Cheve House stood before him. The façade of golden Portland stone welcomed him with memories of his youth. He and Jonathan had often ridden the stone lions on either side of the front door, and there to the north was the larch plantation where Sarah had had to be helped down from the top of the tallest tree.

He was grinning as he handed the reins to a groom, and his hat to the butler. His grin lasted until he stepped into the morning room.

"Adam! At last." His mother came to meet him with a worried face, standing on tiptoe to kiss his cheek. "Jane threw a priceless Ping vase at Bradfield and he said he will never forgive her. Or do I mean Ling?"

"Ming, Mama."

Behind her, his sister burst into torrents of tears. "What shall I do, Adam?" she wailed.

"Choose the Sèvres next time," he advised callously. "You ought to know by now how your husband feels about Chinese porcelain."

"There will not be a next time. He has vowed never to speak to me again. I shall kill myself."

Lady Cheverell rushed to her daughter's side. "You must not say such things, Jane. Adam will go and have a word with Bradfield and straighten matters out between you. There, there, my love."

Jane looked up at Adam with hope in her swimming blue eyes.

"No, really, Mama!" he objected. "I have just arrived and now you want me to dash off to Cheshire. Bradfield will chase down here after her as soon as he gets over his pique and we'd pass on the road, just like last time. I shall wait here until he arrives."

"You unfeeling brute," wept Jane. "I had thought better of you."

Adam had had enough. "I'm tired of being wept at!" he exploded. "Sarah Meade is the only female I know who never enacts me a Cheltenham tragedy."

"You always did like Sarah better than the rest of us," sniffed his sister sulkily.

Lady Cheverell was stunned by his outburst. "Sarah Meade is an exceptional person," she offered in a timid voice.

Her tone reminded him of the way she used to speak to his father when the late viscount was indulging in one of his frequent fits of ill humour. Overcome with remorse, he picked her up and hugged her till she squeaked. She was a tiny woman, always overshadowed by her tall offspring, and now she felt more fragile than ever in his arms.

"I beg your pardon, Mama." He set her down on a brocaded sofa and sat beside her. She reached up to brush back his vagrant lock of hair. "Of course I shall talk to Bradfield, and even go after him if he does not turn up in a couple of days. By the way, Jane, why did you throw the wretched thing in the first place?"

"He insists on calling our firstborn Cyril, after his father, and I cannot abide the name. I am going upstairs to rest." With an air of offended dignity, Lady Bradfield flounced out of the room.

"More hair than wit," snorted her brother. "Oh, Lord, is she breeding at last? You should have told me. I never would have shouted at her like that. I shall have to apologize."

"It was most unlike you, dear. You have always been amazingly patient with your sisters, and I know they can be trying at times. It is quite a relief to me to have married them all off successfully at last."

"Is successfully the correct word?"

"Jane is really very fond of Bradfield. I daresay she will settle down when she has children to care for. She always did grow crotchety when she was bored. But what has thrown *you* in the hips, Adam?"

"Perhaps I am bored, too," he responded lightly.

A gleam entered his mother's eye. "Then I shall recommend the same remedy," she said with unwonted firmness. "It is time you found yourself a bride and set up your nursery."

"Dash it, Mama, I am only twenty-seven, much too young to be leg-shackled. I have years ahead of me before I need worry about producing an heir."

"Yes, dear, but it is you I am concerned about, not your hypercritical heir."

"Hypothetical," he murmured.

"I should so like to see you settled, with a family of your own. Perhaps you would spend more time here at Cheve if you had a wife and children," her ladyship said wistfully.

"I am the most selfish beast in nature! Of course, you must be lonely here with all the girls gone." Once again Adam was filled with remorse. "I had not realized it, but now I know, I shall make a point of coming down more often."

"I did not mean to complain, Adam. Sarah visits me often, and dear Jonathan too, but you know how few close neighbours we have."

"Yes, it is an isolated spot."

She pressed her advantage. "And if I had a daughter-in-law living with me, then I should never be lonely, however much time you spent in London."

"Lord, Mama, that is not the kind of marriage I want! I do not mean to leave my wife languishing in the country while I disport myself in town, as my father did."

Lady Cheverell pounced. "Then you will look about you for a bride? It is the dearest wish of my heart."

"It seems I have talked myself into a corner." He smiled down at her ruefully. "I shall look about me."

"Have you no one in mind?"

"No, but it should not prove too onerous a task. Every Season brings a new crop of delightful young ladies."

"The next Season is nine months away!"

"I am quite content to wait. Surely you do not expect me to make the rounds of all the great houses of Britain in search of love in the meantime?"

"I thought we might have a house party. Your sisters are coming; and they will each be bringing an eligible young lady. Except poor Jane, of course."

"You are a complete hand, Mama! You have been planning this for weeks, at least. Is Jane's trouble only a ruse to bring me here?"

"Certainly not! I cannot deny that I have been making plans, but I did not set a date. Only since you are here already, would this not be a good moment? The girls are all prepared to be here within the week."

"If you insist." Adam sighed in resignation. "I cannot promise to marry any of my sisters' choices, though. I dread to think what sort of young ladies they will consider suitable matches for me."

"Of course you must not marry where you do not feel a decided attachment."

These words brought to Adam's mind three females to whom he had been attached, and who awaited his assistance in London. "I shall have to go back to town for a few days," he warned.

"Will you be able to return by a week tomorrow?"

"That depends on your son-in-law, since I have offered to speak to him when he arrives. Jane has been here for three days? I look to see Bradfield appear today, or tomorrow at the latest. Give me ten days and I engage to be here to greet your guests. You will not object if I bring a

35

couple of friends back from London to support me through this ordeal?"

"Pray do not think of it as an ordeal, Adam, or I shall cancel the whole thing."

He brightened, then his mother's anxious face stiffened his resolve. "I daresay it will be an enjoyable party, and at least it will be pleasant to see Mary and Eliza and Louise. I must go and change out of my dirt now, before I can join you for luncheon. I am devilish sharp-set so I shall not keep you waiting."

As he made his way up the wide, curving stairway, he was struck by a horrid thought. The earliest he could reach London, if he left at first light tomorrow, was late tomorrow evening. Janet, Marguerite and Peggy would have heard nothing from him for three days. He could not imagine what had possessed him to leave them without definite word of his return, and it seemed all too likely that they might decide to follow him into Wiltshire. The possibility of their coming face-to-face with her ladyship was too dreadful to contemplate.

"Gossett!" he bellowed, pausing halfway up the stairs.

A footman who was crossing the hall looked at him in astonishment and broke into a run. A few moments later the butler appeared, hurriedly removing his baize apron.

"Your lordship called?" he enquired, as imperturbable as his brother in London.

"Yes. I must speak to you privately at once, and I need to change. Come up to my chamber with me."

"At once, my lord." Gossett handed his apron to the footman who had fetched him. "Hot water for his lordship immediately," he ordered, then trod in stately fashion up the stairs, no twitch of an eyebrow revealing the least curiosity about this unusual request.

Adam's suite was always kept in a state of readiness since his rare visits were frequently unannounced. The high-ceilinged, airy bedchamber with its huge, Jacobean four-poster, had a lady's boudoir, presently unused, opening off one side, and a gentleman's dressing room off the other. To this latter the viscount now repaired.

He shrugged out of his coat while Gossett, used to his arrival without Wrigley, removed from his wardrobe the garments appropriate to an afternoon in the country.

"Your lordship wished to say?" the butler prompted.

"I am expecting—well, half-expecting—some visitors." Adam wondered how much his London Gossett had revealed to this country Gossett about their master's life of dissipation in town. He pulled off his cravat and unbuttoned his shirt.

"Indeed, my lord?"

A momentary reprieve appeared in the form of a footman bearing a jug of hot water. He was pressed into service to remove his lordship's boots, a task far beneath the dignity of a butler. By the time he left with an armful of soiled clothing and the boots to be polished, Adam had gathered his thoughts.

"Unwanted visitors," he said firmly as he removed the road dust from his person at the basin on the marble washstand. "A young woman, to be precise— or possibly three young women."

"Indeed, my lord." Gossett's voice expressed nothing but mild interest as he handed his master the towel.

"Yes, indeed. When—if—they arrive, they are to be received with the utmost discretion and directed to the vicarage. . . ."

"To the vicarage, my lord?" The butler's eyebrows rose a good eighth of an inch.

"To the vicarage. Before her ladyship sees them. They are to be treated with respect, mind."

"Very good, my lord. Your shirt, my lord."

As Adam donned shirt, buckskins and a glossy pair of top boots, he realised that he must warn the Meades. However, his chères amies were unlikely to arrive on his heels. He would wait until tomorrow, to give Sarah's dudgeon time to fade. Though she had in the end agreed to help him, he was aware she was hurt and angry. The knowledge that never again would he have her unqualified admiration disturbed him more than he was ready to admit.

As he tied his cravat, he made a deliberate effort to change his train of thought.

"I shall spend the afternoon in the estate office," he said. "Send a message to Mr. Brill to say that I should like to see him if he is not otherwise engaged. I am not to be disturbed by anyone else. Unless Miss Meade should call."

"Very good, my lord." Gossett sounded blander than ever.

Adam shot him a suspicious look and quickly added, "Or Mr. Meade. Or Lord Bradfield, I suppose."

"Very good, my lord," the butler repeated, and helped him into his coat.

Chapter Five

<del>+</del> <del>++</del>

"Here's the post, miss." Nellie skipped into the vicarage dining room, laid several letters on the breakfast table at Sarah's elbow, and beamed at her mistress.

"You are in good spirits this morning, Nell."

"Peter's axed me to walk out wi' him come Sunday, miss. Mrs. Hicks says as I can go if 'tis all right wi' the reverend."

Jonathan raised his head from his book.

"Peter?" he asked.

"The groom from Cheve House who fetches the post from Amesbury," Sarah told him. "I believe he is a respectable young man."

"Oh yes, sir, and ever so handsome."

Brother and sister exchanged smiles. "Yes, you may go," said Jonathan, "but do not wander beyond the village street."

"I bain't no Nan Wootton," said the maid indignantly. "You won't see *my* apron to my chin afore I've a ring on me finger."

"Handsome is as handsome does," warned Sarah. She picked up the letters. "Thank you, Nellie. Ask Mrs. Hicks to heat the soup now, if you please. I shall leave in a quarter of an hour. Jonathan, here is a letter from the Bishop, so do not return to your book."

"A letter! This is more like a volume!" The vicar weighed the package in his hand before opening it.

"Yes, it is fortunate that Lady Cheverell has Peter pay the postage as well as fetch the mail from the receiving office, or your Bishop would bankrupt us."

"He is a trifle verbose," her brother conceded. There was silence but for the rustle of paper as he perused the four sheets while Sarah read a short missive from a relative. "What it boils down to," he said at last, "is that he wants to see me in Salisbury tomorrow."

Sarah set aside her letter. "You shall tell me about it later. I must be off, for I told Arthur to have Dapple ready at nine and Goody Newman's soup will grow cold." She kissed the top of his head in passing and went to put on her bonnet.

The little pony was waiting between the gig's shafts when she stepped out of the front door. Mrs. Hicks carefully set the earthenware jar of soup on the floor, well wrapped in straw to keep it hot, and a basket of victuals beside it. Sarah took the reins from Arthur, stepped up into the light carriage, and was soon tooling down the village street, waving to her brother's parishioners.

Goody Newman lived in an isolated cottage a mile or so outside Little Fittleton. The widow of a shepherd, she had been an aged crone as long as Sarah could remember. The village children thought her a witch, and lovelorn youths went to her for potions to charm their sweethearts. She was a bad-tempered old woman, and visiting her was one of Sarah's least enjoyed parish duties.

She was just turning off the road to Cheve House onto a grassy track when Adam hailed her. Glad of company, she was more cordial than she might otherwise have been.

"Good morning," she responded as he rode up beside

the gig. "You are out and about early for a town buck."

"I was coming to see you. Don't tell me you are off to call on the wicked witch?"

"You must not call her that, Adam. You are not a child any longer. Do you remember how frightened of her we used to be?"

"Yes. Jonathan dared me to knock on her door and run away, and I would not do it."

"It must have been the only dare you did not accept. I am a brave woman now and am taking her some soup. Will you come with me?"

"Do I hear a plea in your voice? I think you are as bold as a dunghill cock."

"All crow and no fight? Gammon. She is harmless despite her sharp tongue. However, you could charm a crow from the tree, so if you set your mind to it, you will have her eating from the palm of your hand."

"A revolting mixed metaphor, and I do not take it kindly that you think my charm is to be turned on and off at will. Stop a moment while I hitch Caesar on behind. I shall sit with you so that you need not crane your neck."

She reined in Dapple. "Mind you do not put your foot in the soup," she advised as he jumped up beside her. "It would ruin the polish of your boot."

"I am willing to risk that dreadful fate for the opportunity of being driven in this dashing vehicle by so notable a whip."

Dapple trotted on while Caesar, with his longer stride, walked behind, snorting in disgust.

"Now you are trying to charm the cock from the dunghill, are you?" Sarah asked, smiling. She was still put out with him but he was irresistible in this teasing humour.

"I should not dare." They rounded a bend and the

widow's cottage stood before them. He frowned at the sight. "It needs rethatching. I shall send some men over with barley-straw as soon as the harvest is over."

"The roof does look ragged. I had not noticed." If she could not remain aloof from his teasing, his consideration for a useless old woman was still more difficult to ignore. "Here, you take the basket, for you are certain to spill the soup."

"Do you think me so clumsy?" His tone was light, but she heard a double meaning in his words and avoided his eye.

"No," she said. "I trust you to knock on the door without dropping the basket."

"And without running away," he added, suiting action to the words.

While she tidied the cottage's single room, not an arduous task as Lady Cheverell paid a village woman to come in once a week to clean, Sarah listened to Adam bewitching the witch. He coaxed Goody Newman into admitting that the soup was delicious, the weather excellent, and Sarah a pretty and kind young lady. Since the crone usually complained that the soup was tasteless, swore that the weather, however warm, was bad for her bones, and twitted Sarah on being an ape leader, this was a miracle indeed.

Sarah was both amused and disgusted at how easily it was accomplished. She recognized herself in Goody Newman, another victim of the viscount's charm.

"Well?" he challenged as Dapple pulled them willingly back along the track. "Did I pass the test?"

"You exerted yourself to please," she accused him.

"Should I have exerted myself to offend? She might have turned us into black beetles."

"Surely Prince Charming is always turned into a frog?"

"I should not mind in the least, if I could guarantee that it would be you who turned me back again."

Sarah felt her cheeks grow hot. She shook the reins, surprising Dapple into a canter for a few yards. Adam clutched at the side of the gig in exaggerated terror. His colour, too, was considerably heightened. Sarah supposed he must be embarrassed to be caught flirting with the vicar's sister.

She turned the talk to parish matters which he, as landlord, ought to be conversant with. There was a hint of constraint between them.

When they reached the vicarage he helped her down from the carriage. Arthur came to take charge of Dapple and Caesar. Sarah was about to step through the open front door when Adam's hand on her arm stopped her.

He looked down at her, his blue eyes serious. "Have I offended you?" he asked.

"Don't talk such fustian," she said gaily, fixing her gaze on his waistcoat buttons. "I am no schoolroom miss. Come in. Jonathan will be pleased to see you."

Adam followed her into the hall, feeling like a singularly clumsy frog. Sarah was his friend, not one of the flirtatious debutantes regularly flung at his head by matchmaking mamas. He had already lost her good opinion; if he did not watch his step he would lose her friendship, too. In a sombre mood he joined Jonathan in the study while Sarah went up to put off her bonnet. They discussed the parish business Sarah had broached, until she looked in to ask if he would care to stay to luncheon.

Her tone was reserved. Adam hesitated, for the first time in his life uncertain of his welcome in this house. He suddenly recalled the original purpose of his visit.

"Do stay," urged Jonathan, "unless her ladyship is particularly expecting you."

"Thank you, I will. Though you may regret your invitation when I tell you what I have done."

"Nothing you have done could make me regret your company," said the vicar gently.

Sarah was regarding Adam with a wary expression. However, she turned back to the hall and called, "Nellie, tell Mrs. Hicks his lordship will stay to luncheon."

Then she stepped into the study, closed the door firmly behind her, and took a seat close to her brother. They both looked at their guest expectantly.

Adam rarely found himself at a loss for words, but now he fumbled for an explanation. How could he have thought to send his lightskirts to the vicarage? He did not want his mother to see them, yet he had been ready to insult Sarah with their presence. His thoughtlessness was inexcusable.

"Perhaps Sarah had best leave," suggested Jonathan.

Adam grimaced, studying his linked hands. "No," he said wryly, "let her know the worst of me." He explained his instructions to his butler. "It was presumptuous of me," he admitted. "My wits must have gone begging. I shall have Gossett direct them to the George at Amesbury and tell them I shall join them there in due course."

He looked up. Jonathan was grinning at him in open amusement.

"Your wits have gone begging for trouble," he said. "Surely it is not at all likely that they will come all this way after you, instead of awaiting your return. They must know that you will not abandon them."

"Perhaps they have less faith in Adam than you do, Jonathan," his sister pointed out, with a voice and expression devoid of feeling. "Be that as it may, if they do come it would be unkind to make them go all the way back to Amesbury without any certainty of assistance. Let them come here and I shall do what I can for them."

"You ought to be outraged at my effrontery," said Adam softly.

"Much good that would do. Besides, they are no worse than poor Nan Wootton, and no more deserving of my indifference. Pray excuse me. I must go and help Mrs. Hicks."

The gentlemen rose. Adam's gaze followed Sarah as she left the room, dignity and grace in every line of her slender figure. There was a curious lump in his throat. He turned to find Jonathan watching him.

"She is a remarkable woman, my sister, is she not?" the vicar observed.

The viscount nodded, momentarily unable to speak.

In the kitchen, Mrs. Hicks was stirring a custard when Sarah arrived.

"His lordship allus liked a gooseberry fool, as I recall," she said. "I sent Nellie to pick the berries, though I'll have to throw half on 'em out, I make no doubt, for she'll pick the ripe wi' the green and see no difference."

"I'll go and help her, unless there is something else you'd prefer me to do."

"Nay, off wi' you, Miss Sarah, and send the good-for-nothing back here to chop onions. I'm making mutton pasties wi' the leavin's o' leg, and there's some o' Goody Newman's soup left, and a nice pair o' trout I were saving to the reverend's dinner."

"Of course his lordship's superior claim to the trout is indisputable," Sarah commented wryly.

"That Peter bought 'em in Amesbury just this morning. Caught fresh yesterday in the Avon, they was."

"Currying favour with Nellie, is he? How useful it is to have a pretty maidservant."

"Currying favour wi' me, more like, so's I'll put in a good word for him wi' the master."

Sarah laughed, and went off down the garden. It was warm and peaceful among the gooseberry bushes, with bees humming mightily around the red- and blackcurrant blossom nearby. She would have liked to dawdle, letting the sun bake out her irritable dissatisfaction even if it scattered freckles on her nose, but the fuzzy berries must be cooked and it was already near noon. That wretched man! Here was Mrs. Hicks scurrying to make his favourite dish even though she had probably not passed more than three words with him in a decade!

At least he had the grace to acknowledge that his behaviour was dastardly.

Mrs. Hicks, pink-cheeked from the heat of the oven and the compliments on her trout with green peas, had carried in the crisp, golden mutton pasties when Adam mentioned his mother's house party.

"She and the girls are in league to marry me off," he said, laughing. "Louise and Mary and Eliza are each to bring an eligible maiden for me to choose among."

"Must you select just one?" asked Sarah sharply. "I wonder you do not mean to wed them all, like a Mussulman. But they are allowed *four* wives, are they not, as well as any number of concubines. Jane will have to find you another."

Adam and Jonathan looked as startled by her outburst as she was herself.

"My dear . . ." her brother began with an air of reproof.

Sarah pushed back her chair. "I beg your pardon," she whispered, and fled the room.

Chapter Six

Jonathan left early the next morning for the drive into Salisbury which, at Dapple's pace, would take him a couple of hours.

Since that horrid moment at the luncheon table, he had treated Sarah as if she were made of glass. Even when she apologized to him for her shocking rudeness to a guest, he had not breathed a word of reproach.

"My poor dear," was all he said, enfolding her in his arms.

She rested her forehead against his shoulder. "Did he . . . did Adam guess that I am jealous? He must have done so. I shall never be able to face him again."

"No, he blamed himself for oversetting your nerves. I had a hard time persuading him not to change his orders to Gossett. I know you will want to do what you can for those unfortunate females."

At that time, Sarah had thought how difficult it was trying to live up to her saintly brother's idealistic view of her. Now, waving goodbye to him as he drove down the street, she was glad he had not let Adam countermand his instructions. She was forced to acknowledge, to herself at least, that she was excessively curious to see what a fashionable Cyprian was like.

The day passed with painful slowness. Every time there

was a sound in the street outside Sarah paused in her chores, half hoping, half dreading that it might be Adam. Discovering that she had set the cuff on the sleeve the wrong way round, she gave up trying to concentrate on hemming a shirt for Jonathan. She decided to go for a walk to ease her restlessness, but when she looked out of the French windows she saw that while her thoughts had been elsewhere, a pall of grey clouds had crept across the sky. A gusty wind was blowing a haze of chalky dust from the dry fields.

She took from the shelves one of her favourite books, a translation of Herodotus's *Histories,* and went to sit in the front parlour where she could see into the street.

She had not been there long when an elegant travelling carriage approached from the direction of Cheve House. The road through the village came to an end at the viscount's front door, so either Lady Cheverell had had a visitor or the driver had lost his way.

To Sarah's astonishment the carriage with its team of four perfectly matched black horses pulled up before the vicarage. The only explanation she could think of was that it carried one of Adam's lights-o'-love, but she had never dreamed that females of that sort might possess such an extravagant equipage. If Adam treated all his mistresses with similar generosity, it seemed probable that he would shortly find himself with pockets to let.

A smart footman jumped down from the back of the carriage, ran up to the door, and knocked.

Sarah rushed to the mirror over the fireplace and made a vain attempt to tidy her hair. She heard the sound of voices in the hall, then Mrs. Hicks came in.

"A Mrs. Goudge to see the reverend," she announced, giving Sarah a handsomely engraved card. "I told the fella as he's not at home."

"Mrs. Henry Goudge," Sarah read. That was the name of the first ladybird Adam had mentioned, the one whose husband was lost at sea. She felt an unexpected rush of sympathy. "I shall see her, Mrs. Hicks. Show her in here, if you please."

It took all her resolution not to peer out of the window like a vulgar busybody, to see what sort of creature was descending from that magnificent carriage.

The woman who entered the parlour moments later could not have been less like what she expected. Her black bombazine carriage dress was elegant but plain, trimmed with jet beads, and she was definitely a trifle on the plump side. When she raised her veil her face was white and tired, her dark eyes red-rimmed, and she looked to be at least thirty.

"It is good in you to receive me, ma'am," she said. Her voice was low, with a refined accent that sounded quite natural. "I am at my wits' end or I should not have dreamed of troubling you."

Sarah went to her with both hands held out and led her to a chair. "You must be exhausted after your journey," she said gently. "Do you put off your bonnet and I shall order refreshments." She went to the door, where she found Mrs. Hicks chasing Nellie from her position at the keyhole.

"I'll bring tea, shall I, miss?" the cook enquired. "There's some nice Queen cakes fresh from the oven."

"That will do very well." Sarah closed the door and went back to take a seat opposite her visitor.

Mrs. Goudge was twisting a handkerchief in her kid-gloved hands. Beneath a white lace bonnet-cap her ringlets were raven black, making Sarah feel her own dark brown hair to be utterly insipid. The woman's face was slightly flushed as she said, "I don't know quite how to explain why I am here."

"Lord Cheverell has told me something of your difficulties," Sarah informed her, feeling her own anger rising at Adam's callous seduction and abandonment of this unfortunate woman. "I collect that your husband is reported lost at sea."

Mrs. Goudge raised her handkerchief to dab at her eyes. "I don't know what I shall do without Henry," she said simply. "He was the best of husbands."

Sarah was taken aback. She had supposed that a wife who betrayed her husband must dislike him, but the woman sounded perfectly sincere. Fortunately Mrs. Hicks carried in a tray at that moment, giving her time to reorganize her thoughts.

"I fear there is little I can do for you," she said as she poured the tea, "except send a message to Ad—to his lordship to tell him that you are here."

"The butler promised to inform him. He is out riding, I understand."

"It was wicked of him to desert you at such a moment."

"Oh no, you must not think ill of Adam, Miss Meade. His London butler said he had an urgent summons from Lady Cheverell, and of course his family must come first. It was foolish of me to follow him, but I was distraught."

"He ought not to have . . . led you astray in the first place. Forgive me, but I do not perfectly understand how, if you love your husband, you could have let Adam take advantage of you. I cannot believe he forced himself upon you."

"Heavens, no! I was lonely, you see. I missed Henry desperately. I was standing on Blackfriars Bridge, looking down the river to the docks and wishing that he was on his way back, when Adam drove past. He was afraid that I meant to do away with myself. He was so very kind, Miss Meade. The City merchants tend to ignore females, and I had never met a proper gentleman before. He began to call quite often, to cheer me, and . . . one thing led to another. Indeed you must not blame Adam. When you marry, perhaps you will understand better."

"Perhaps," said Sarah dubiously. She took refuge in the social niceties. "Will you take another cup of tea?"

Mrs. Goudge complimented her on the Queen cakes and they chatted for a while about domestic matters, quite as if Adam's mistress was a respectable village matron. When Mrs. Hicks came in to remove the tray, Sarah passed on the praise of her baking and she beamed and curtsied.

The visitor consulted the watch pinned to the front of her dress.

"I must not take up any more of your time," she said. "If you will be so good as to direct me to a respectable hostelry where I can await Lord Cheverell, I shall be on my way."

"I had almost forgot we were waiting for Adam," said Sarah, not quite truthfully, hoping the set-down would reach that gentleman's ears. "I expect he will be here soon. You must not leave. If you would like to tidy yourself, I shall take you up to the spare chamber."

They went above stairs together, but a certain constraint had fallen between them again at the reminder of Mrs. Goudge's situation.

Sarah wandered down to the study. The emotion uppermost in her mind was confusion. She needed a period of uninterrupted contemplation to sort out her feelings and this was clearly not the right time to attempt that task. She allowed herself a brief flash of envy: if Adam admired black ringlets and a voluptuous figure, why could not she have been so endowed?

She picked up the shirt she had been sewing earlier and went back to the parlour. When Mrs. Goudge returned, she was stitching composedly.

The India merchant's wife was no longer pale and tear-stained. Sarah was surprised that merely washing her face had so effectively removed the ravages of misery and a tiring journey. Then she realised that the woman had used powder, and even a touch of rouge. It was so delicately done that she would never have guessed had she not seen her before its application.

She was staring rudely. She dropped her eyes, flushing, and an awkward silence fell between them.

It was broken by the rumble of wheels in the street, halting at the door. A volley of knocks followed, then Mrs. Hicks's raised voice.

Mrs. Goudge reached for her bonnet and her reticule. "Your visitors must not see me," she said. "Where shall I go?"

"Let us first wait and see who it is," advised Sarah, frowning. It was not like her cook-housekeeper to raise such a rumpus.

Mrs. Hicks appeared in the doorway, scarlet-faced and with a militant glint in her eye.

" 'Tes a young *person*, miss, as had the cheek to tell me to pay off her chaise!"

"Did she give her name?" Sarah enquired.

Mrs. Hicks was opening her mouth to answer when a startling vision pushed past her. Clad in a clinging, décolleté gown of pea-green satin embellished with cherry bows, the new arrival had a willowy figure that curved generously in the right places. A matching bonnet topped flaming red hair above a face painted white, with cerise on the high cheekbones. Her eyelids were blue and her soot-black eyelashes of an improbable length. Sarah developed a sudden admiration for Mrs. Goudge's ability with cosmetics.

Her opinion of Adam's taste took a plunge, but perhaps he always saw the creature by candlelight. This, she was sure, was his opera singer.

"You!" cried Marguerite dramatically, pointing with one hand at Mrs. Goudge while the other rose in a histrionic gesture to her forehead. "Whatcher doing 'ere?"

"The same as you, no doubt," said Mrs. Goudge dryly.

"And oo's she?" The actress turned her attention to Sarah.

"Miss Meade is the vicar's sister."

"And I'm the King's gran'ma! Adam's country piece, are you, ducky? Nothing to be ashamed of, yer in good company. Speakin' o' the devil, where is 'e? Ol' starchy-britches up at the big 'ouse sent me 'ere to see 'im."

Sarah had lost her tongue, so Mrs. Goudge came to the rescue.

"Adam is out riding," she said in a cold voice. "No doubt he will come as soon as he can."

"That's just fine, that is. Oo's gonna pay my carridge, is what I want to know."

Sarah rallied. "I am sure Adam—his lordship—will pay the coachman when he arrives, but perhaps you should not turn it away until you discover whether you still need it. There is no inn in the village."

"My, you do talk nice," said Marguerite admiringly. She looked around the room. "Kind of shabby place 'e's set you up in though, ain't it? You didn't ought to let a gentleman get away wiv it like that, ducks. I'll 'ave a word wiv 'im about it if you like. Swimming in mint sauce, 'e is. You don't 'ave to be shy about asking for nice stuff. After all, 'e gets what 'e wants, don't 'e?" She winked.

"I really am the vicar's sister," said Sarah in desperation, hovering between laughter and tears at the woman's persistent misapprehension. There was no point in taking offence at her frankness. "My brother is in Salisbury calling on the Bishop. He will be back shortly."

"Calling on the Bishop!" The actress mimicked her voice. "La, I vow I am almost ready to believe it."

"It is *true!*" Sarah and Mrs. Goudge assured her as one.

"Then what's Adam think 'e's doing, foisting the likes of me and 'er on a gentry mort?" Marguerite was indignant. "Don't tell me ol' starchy-britches done it wivout 'is orders."

"No, Lord Cheverell told his butler to send you here. He did not want his mother to meet . . . He was protecting his mother. My brother and I have known him since we were children. Of course he could not guess that Mr. Meade would be from home when you arrived. In fact, he did not really believe that you would come."

"Damned—beg parding—deuced if I know why I did. 'Is lordship's not one to let a girl down. Just couldn't stand that Clorinda crowing over me. Clorinda, I don't think. Bertha she were christened and Bertha she'll be buried." She grinned. "And you'll be wondering what I was christened. Well, it weren't Marguerite, but Margaret ain't so different."

"Since you never introduced yourself, I for one was not wondering anything of the sort," said Mrs. Goudge tartly.

" 'Sright, I never did. Well, Marguerite's me stage name and it'll 'ave to do. And I'm sure I beg parding, miss, if I said aught out of line."

Sarah was perfectly willing to let bygones be bygones. She was revising her opinion of Adam's opera singer. To be sure, she was shockingly vulgar in speech and dress, but she was able to laugh at herself and her apology was unforced and apparently sincere. That was not to say that Sarah wanted to entertain her for the next several hours.

Adam had landed her in this bumblebath. Where was the dratted man when she needed him?

Chapter Seven

The pounding of hooves in the village street followed by a thunderous knocking at the front door sent Marguerite rushing to the window. Sarah and Mrs. Goudge kept their dignity and their seats but both looked at her eagerly.

"Cor lumme, it's 'im," announced the actress. "Is me 'air on straight?" With a gliding gait quite unlike her previous sprightly movements, she went to a sofa and disposed herself on it, in an attitude of languorous grace. "Mustn't let 'im know we was all agog, must we," she added.

Sarah briefly considered escaping into the hall to confront Adam on his own, but she wanted to see his expression when he found her sitting with his mistresses as if they were everyday callers. She wished Mrs. Hicks, whose raised voice was once more heard, had not removed the tea tray, that symbol of respectability.

The viscount came into the parlour unannounced, looking sheepish. His eye fell on Marguerite, who had carefully selected the sofa opposite the door.

"Adam darling," she cooed.

"Marguerite!" he exclaimed in a harassed voice and glanced round the room. "Janet. Sarah."

"Miss Meade," the vicar's sister said frostily.

"I beg your pardon, Miss Meade," he apologized, and bowed to her. "If I might have a word with you in private?"

"Pray excuse us, ladies," said Sarah. "We shall not keep you waiting long." She led Adam into the study and turned to face him. "Well?"

"I never intended that you should entertain them," he protested, running his fingers through his hair.

"No, I daresay I should have shut them in together and left them to scratch one another's eyes out," she said with composure. "They are not fond of each other, you know. Marguerite was sadly taken aback to find Mrs. Goudge Janet, is it?—here before her. She was most kind to me, however, and advised me to insist that you buy me more elegant furnishings."

"She what?" He looked blank.

"She was under the impression that I am your 'country piece'. I take it that means what I think it means?"

"Probably," Adam said ruefully. "No, certainly. I'm sorry, Sarah." He took both her hands in his and squeezed them gently.

A tingling sensation raced up her arms, leaving her shaken and breathless. She pulled her hands from his grasp and turned away, praying that he had noticed nothing amiss.

With careful nonchalance she said wryly, "Such is life in a rural vicarage. You will never guess what she called Gossett."

"Tell me." His voice sounded constricted, as if he too were having trouble breathing.

"Old starchy-britches."

He made a choking noise and she swung round. Their eyes met, and both burst into peals of laughter.

"Not a word of this must reach Gossett's ears," he gasped as their mirth died down. "His dignity would be irreparably injured. Yours, however—" he grew serious "—is too much an innate part of you to suffer. All the same, I am truly sorry to have put you in such a position. Am I forgiven?"

"Not quite. I do not want to give you too great an opinion of your ability to charm me into condoning this disgraceful business. Adam, I can do nothing for the two of them. You must take them back to London and deal with their problems there."

"I know it. If only Bradfield would put in an appearance!"

"Surely it is time he and Jane learned to solve their differences without your assistance. Jonathan thinks it unhealthy that Jane runs home to Cheve House whenever she quarrels with her husband. She will never grow up as long as she finds refuge there. It is not as if he beats her, after all."

"No, though I am sure I should if I were her husband rather than her brother. I cannot like to abandon her, however, even if I had not as good as promised Mama that I will deal with Bradfield."

"You cannot abandon *me!*" Sarah was growing angry. "Really, Adam, what am I supposed to do with your ladyloves while you dance attendance on your sister? They will never leave if you do not go with them."

The viscount looked unconvinced. Sarah was marshalling fresh arguments when the door knocker resounded for the fourth time that busy afternoon.

"I suppose this is the third," she said in disgust.

Mrs. Hicks's footsteps were followed by a high voice that cried in country accents, "Help me! Oh, quickly, let me come in."

"That's Peggy all right," said Adam, heading for the hall.

Sarah followed him in time to see a distraught girl, modestly dressed in blue muslin, throw herself into his arms.

"What is it, pet?" he asked, then looked up as a large young man pushed past Mrs. Hicks at the open front door.

The intruder pulled the girl away from Adam and without a word swung at him with both fists. One hit him in the pit of the stomach; the second caught him in the face as he doubled over, and stretched him gasping on the floor. His assailant stood back with a satisfied air, hands on hips, still speechless.

Peggy dropped to her knees at Adam's side, wailing and wringing her hands. Mrs. Goudge and Marguerite dashed out of the parlour and joined her, heedless of the damage to their finery. Mrs. Goudge produced her wisp of lace handkerchief and applied it to his bloody nose.

"Cold water and clean linen," Sarah instructed Mrs. Hicks calmly.

Marguerite jumped to her feet and advanced on the hapless youth, who was by now looking confused at the sudden eruption of feminine pulchritude. She seized a handful of shirtfront and shook her finger in his face, berating him in a furious voice. Sarah tried not to laugh.

Mrs. Hicks returned with water and cloths. She set them on the floor beside his lordship, where Janet and Peggy were making soothing noises and trying in vain to stanch the copious flow of blood.

"Leave them to it," Sarah advised the housekeeper. "I think you might rescue that young fellow and take him off to the kitchen, little as I approve of his action. Try to keep him in the house, though. I want Mr. Meade to talk to him." She noticed her maid gaping from the stairs. "And send Nellie about her business. It is crowded enough in here."

She turned back to Adam. He had recovered his breath and was struggling to evade his nurses.

"Let be go," he said in a muffled voice. "I'll show hib I dow a thig or two about fisticuffs whed I'b dot attacked without fair wardig."

"Don't you dare sit up," Sarah ordered sternly. "You will ruin the carpet."

Mrs. Goudge looked at her, shocked at her callousness. "If you have an old sheet to cover the sofa, Miss Meade, we can carry him into the parlour. He will be much more comfortable there than on the floor."

His lordship was understood to say that he was damned if a bunch of females was going to carry him anywhere. He was quite capable of walking, and undertook, with the aid of a large square of linen, to prevent his lifeblood from staining the rug. He threw a reproachful glance at Sarah.

The young man had been led away by Mrs. Hicks, so Sarah relented. Marguerite and Mrs. Goudge supported Adam on either side while Peggy followed with the bowl of water, now pinkish, and the rest of the cloths. He subsided in a reclining position on the sofa, his women fussing over him.

Sarah would not for the world have admitted it, but she was impressed by their devotion to him. Nothing of that appeared on her face, however, when she said, "Lord Cheverell and I have not quite finished our business, ladies. Perhaps you would not mind waiting in the hall for a few minutes?"

Reluctantly they filed out, Mrs. Goudge leading the way and Peggy last again, with many a backward glance. Sarah sat down and shook her head reprovingly at the viscount.

"You're laughig at be," accused Adam.

She smiled. "It was quite funny, though I daresay I

should more properly have indulged in a fit of hysterics. Your nose is swelling. You cannot possibly present yourself to Lady Cheverell in that state."

"He darkened my daylights, or one of them, as well as drawing my cork," he said gloomily, probing his cheek with cautious fingers. "I shall not be fit to appear in public for at least a week."

"Darkened your daylights?"

"Gave me a black eye. It was a glancing blow."

"You will have to borrow some of Marguerite's face powder," Sarah scoffed. "I suggest you take her and Mrs. Goudge down to Amesbury tonight. Write a note to your mother making your excuses and Arthur shall take it up to the house. They can send a groom to the George with your things. Old starchy-britches will see to it."

They exchanged grins and Adam said, "Oh, very well. You are in the right of it as usual. Only promise me that as soon as I am gone you will do your best to persuade Peggy's Billy not to let fly with the wisty castors on sight of me in future."

"I promise, but I must warn you that I shall try to effect a reconciliation between them."

"Are you afraid that I shall cut up stiff at losing my convenient? I assure you it is not so. In fact, I engage to provide a respectable portion for the child if you can persuade the lad to marry her."

"I have little doubt of managing that, judging by his actions. However, she may be more difficult to convince. She adores you, Adam."

He grimaced. "Do your best," he urged. "I mean to sever the connection in any event. If she does not wish to wed him, I shall provide for her in some other way."

"You really care for them, don't you? All of them."

"They all depend on me, you see. Even Marguerite, though she will soon enough find a new protector."

"You mean to give up your mistresses when you marry?"

"How can I expect a wife to be faithful if I am not?"

"I like you, Adam. Now you stay there and I shall fetch pen and paper so you may write to her ladyship. You are an unconscionable rogue but I do like you."

She stooped to drop a fleeting kiss on his unbruised cheek as she passed him.

Surprised and touched by this gesture of friendship, Adam watched Sarah go. Though her round gown of fawn cambric, modestly embellished with drawn-thread-work, could not conceal her graceful figure, it did nothing to enhance it. He had a sudden wish to see her in silks and laces. The house party at Cheve, he decided, must be the occasion for a grand ball.

He was permitted no leisure for further contemplation. As soon as Sarah opened the door into the hall, Marguerite, Janet and Peggy surged through it, throwing black looks at one another. Tired of basking under their ministrations, Adam hastily sat up. To his relief, his nose did not start bleeding again, but the sudden movement revived the ache in his abdomen where Billy's first punch had landed. He tried to breathe shallowly.

"Janet, Marguerite, I shall escort you back to London tomorrow," he announced. "Your carriages are both waiting in the street. Go to the George at Amesbury and I shall join you shortly."

They glared at each other but departed without protest. He heard them making their farewells to Sarah in the hall, then she came in with writing materials.

"Be quick," she said. "Mrs. Hicks is having difficulty restraining Billy."

Peggy began to weep. "You're leavin' me behind wi' him," she sobbed.

"Miss Meade will take care of you," he said helplessly. "I shall return in a week at most. Be a good girl, pet."

"I want to be wi' you, Adam."

"Come along, now, Peggy," said Sarah with a gentle firmness Adam had to admire. "His lordship needs quiet to compose his letter. Nellie shall take you above stairs to wash your face before you say goodbye to him."

"Me bag's in the pony trap, miss," said the girl docilely, recognizing the voice of authority. "I hired it at the George but I didn't pay the driver yet."

"We shall see to that first. Did you come on the Exeter stage?"

"Yes, miss. Billy were outside and me inside. He didn't have the blunt to hire a horse in Amesbury so he walked. Fancy him arriving just when I did." Her tone was admiring, Adam was glad to note, though she did add, "O' course I drove all the way to Adam's house and back." She followed Sarah out, chattering about her journey.

Adam racked his brains for an excuse to present to his mother for deserting her without ceremony. Then he remembered that two days hence in the House of Lords, Lord Lansdowne was to present a loyal address to the Prince Regent on the subject of the abolition of slavery. It was an important occasion, at which Tsar Alexander of Russia and King Frederick of Prussia might be present. He had told the marquis he would try to be there to support him, so to inform Lady Cheverell that he had promised to attend was merely stretching the truth a little. He scribbled a note.

Sarah returned. "I am not sure it is wise to expose Nellie to Peggy," she said, frowning. "Nell has nothing but scorn for poor Nan Wootton, but being left with child by an inconstant soldier and being supported in style by a lord are two different matters."

"Make sure that she hears the first part of Peggy's story and I guarantee she won't be running off to the gold-paved streets of London. By the way, though I expect you can count on Mrs. Hicks's discretion, will you be able to stop Nellie spreading the story of this day's doings?"

"By now the whole village is discussing Mrs. Goudge and Marguerite," said Sarah wryly. "They were not precisely inconspicuous, you know. I'll see that Nell does not talk about Peggy, though, for it would sadly discomfit the poor child if she weds her Billy."

"I was not concerned for Peggy's comfort as much as yours. However, it is my reputation that will be ripped to shreds, I make no doubt."

"Such carryings-on are expected of gentlemen. I daresay even your mama will be shocked only because I was induced to consort with your lightskirts."

"Sarah, I . . ."

"I'm sorry, Adam, that was not fair of me. You have already apologized and I do not mean to carp at you forever. I am a little tired."

"Of course. I'll take myself off at once." He stood up. "Just tell me, did you not say that Nan Wootton had a follower at the George?"

"Yes, Jem. He's an ostler."

"Then while you are exerting your powers of persuasion on Billy, I shall have a go at Jem. Perhaps we can make it a double wedding."

Those intriguing sparks of gold in her eyes glowed as she smiled at him.

"Jonathan has spoken to him, but I imagine the persuasive powers of religion are as nothing to those of the pocket-book," she said demurely.

"Nan shall have a dowry," he promised. He raised her hand to his lips, returning her earlier casual kiss with interest. She had beautiful hands, he noticed, slender but strong. The skin was slightly roughened from her work in kitchen and garden.

He would bring her some Denmark Lotion from town. Some ladies might be insulted that he thought they needed it, but Sarah was too sensible. She would accept it as a gift of friendship.

In spite of everything, she liked him. Smiling, he touched his fingertip to the precise spot on his cheek which her lips had brushed.

Chapter Eight

<+- +>

Drawn against her will, Sarah moved to the parlour window. The back of her hand was pressed to her cheek, as if Adam's kiss might be transferred from one to the other. Half hidden by the flowered chintz curtain, she watched him mount Caesar.

She saw him glance toward the window and tip his glossy beaver to her, then ride off down the street in the direction of Amesbury. Town beau though he was, he looked magnificent on horseback, sitting straight and proud with an easy command of the splendid gelding. At this distance the damage to his face was invisible.

Sarah sighed, squared her weary shoulders and went to deal with the problems the errant viscount had left behind him.

Billy sat at the kitchen table drinking ale, while Mrs. Hicks bustled about him in the midst of her preparations for dinner. A large, stolid-looking young man in the dress of a respectable groom, he stumbled to his feet as Sarah entered the kitchen, wiping his mouth with his hand.

"I see that Mrs. Hicks is looking after you," said Sarah brightly. "Will you do me a small favour? I need my manservant, Arthur, to run an errand. He is somewhere about the garden or stable so it will not be hard to find him."

"No need to call him, I s'll run your errand, miss," he said gruffly.

She smiled at him. "It is kind in you to offer, but I want to send him to Cheve House. I daresay you will not like to go there."

Billy turned crimson. "I s'll do it for *you*, miss, not for *him*."

"Thank you." She gave him Adam's notes and described how to reach the servants' entrance at Cheve. "You will return here, won't you?" she added. "I have no right to give you orders, but I want very much to talk to you, and so will the vicar when he comes home."

His nod was noncommittal, but Sarah thought it more likely that he would stay close to Peggy rather than chase off after the viscount. She turned to Mrs. Hicks.

The cook-housekeeper was beating veal cutlets, her fierce expression suggesting that something other than food was on her mind.

"That man!" she uttered as Billy left the kitchen. "Ca's hisself a gentleman!"

"Billy calls himself a gentleman?" Sarah pretended to misunderstand. "I am sure you must be mistaken."

Mrs. Hicks snorted. " 'Tes not that jobberknowl I mean, missy, and well you knows it. Bringing his fancy pieces into this house, the cheek o' him!"

"He could not let them meet her ladyship," said Sarah placatingly.

"Oh, aye, he's brung you round his thumb a'ready, ha'n't he? He c'd talk the hind leg offn a donkey, that one."

"He is conscious of having acted badly, I assure you. He said that he knows he can rely on your discretion not to spread the tale in the village."

67

"His lordship said that, did he? Well, soft sawder butters no parsnips."

Her voice was tart but she looked pleased. Wondering at Adam's ability to exert his charm even at a distance, Sarah went to find Peggy.

She decided to interview the girl in Jonathan's study. After all, it was parish business of a sort, for Adam was a parishioner. Seated behind the desk, she could almost pretend that Peggy was just another farmer's daughter caught tumbling in the hay with her sweetheart on a summer evening. That was a situation she was used to dealing with.

Peggy's tear-stained face was apprehensive.

"I do not mean to scold," Sarah said gently. "Lord Cheverell has told me something of your history. Will you tell me how your troubles all came about?"

There was a certain note of nostalgia in the girl's voice when she talked about the dull routine of the rural manor where she had been a housemaid. The fabled wonders of London had held an irresistible attraction. Running off in search of excitement, the country innocent had found more than she had bargained for.

Sarah was appalled at Peggy's halting description of the brothel where she had been incarcerated. As soon as the madam ceased to lock her door, thinking her spirit broken, she had escaped, but lost in the great city, penniless, she had soon been found. Adam had come upon her just in time to save her from being dragged back. Like an avenging angel, he had turned the woman's whip on her and her bully, then he and Peggy had run before she could return with help.

Peggy's face glowed as she spoke of Adam's heroism, of his solicitude for her. He had tried to persuade her to return to her home.

"But I knowed the mistress'd never have me back. 'Sides, I couldn't face Billy arter leaving him like that. I wanted to thank Adam and I on'y knowed one way to do it. First off, he wouldn't have me. I thought I weren't good enow for him and I got downright mopish and he were comforting me, like, and . . . well, a man ain't a stone. Oh, miss, he were that kind and gentle. I never knowed it could be like that."

Sarah felt a blush stealing up her cheeks, but not for the world would she stop the flow of artless confidences. She murmured a word of encouragement.

"The best of 'em," Peggy went on, "the ones that don't hurt you, they don't care how you feel just so's they feel good. Adam's different. He reely cares if you enjoy it. When I was living in Chelsea, I talked to some of the other girls. There's lots of gentlemen have villas in Chelsea for their convenients. I reckon there's not one in a hundred like Adam, as tries to make you feel good. Course, a respectable lady like you wouldn't understand, miss. A gentleman don't expect his wife to get any pleasure from it. 'Twouldn't be proper."

If Sarah's face had grown any hotter, it would have burst into flame. She attempted to change the subject.

"Billy must love you greatly to have kept searching till he found you."

"D'you think so, miss? I know I oughta marry Billy, if he'll have me, but he's a simple fellow. He won't try to please me, nor won't know how."

"Could you not teach him?"

"Like as not he wouldn't listen."

Sarah found herself back at the same subject. It was not one she could broach with Billy.

"I'll see if the vicar will talk to him," she suggested

doubtfully. She was afraid that Jonathan's knowledge might be as meagre as her own. "Is that the only objection you have to marrying him?"

"I want to stay wi' Adam!"

"Lord Cheverell intends to take a bride soon."

"That won't make a ha'p'orth o' difference," said Peggy cynically.

"He says it will. He told me he does not mean to keep a mistress once he is wed."

The girl's face fell and she bit her lip. "Well, he's not like the others, so maybe he won't. Is he going to marry you, miss?"

With great difficulty, Sarah kept her countenance. "He is to choose among several young ladies visiting Cheve House. I fear you must face the fact that his association with you is at an end, my dear. He will make fair provision for you if you will not have Billy, or give you a dowry if you will. Which is it to be? It is useless for me to try to persuade Billy to forgive you if you do not mean to accept him."

"You reely think he loves me?"

"Can you think of any other reason for a servant to risk transportation by attacking a peer?"

"He's a plucky lad a' right, ain't he?" Peggy was convinced. "I'll wed him if he'll have me. On'y I wisht I was a grand young lady, fit for his lordship's bride." She sighed.

"I am sure you have made the right decision. Now, you had best spend the night with Nellie, and in the morning we shall consider what is to be done next."

"You're as kind as he is, miss. There's plenty o' ladies wouldn't even let me speak to their maids."

"I rely on you to persuade her that running away to London is not a good idea. Off you go, now, and tell Mrs. Hicks I wish to see Billy as soon as he returns."

Sarah hoped for a few minutes alone to decide on her approach to the young groom, but he came in almost at once.

"You were very quick," she said.

" 'Tain't fur, and I were in a hurry to see where his lordship lives. 'Tis a mighty fancy house. No wonder he won over my Peggy wi' his fine gifts and promises."

"That is not at all what happened," Sarah assured him. She fixed her eyes on her clasped hands and somehow managed not to blush as she repeated to the young man the shocking story she had heard from Adam and Peggy.

"She told me as he rescued her," he said doubtfully. "I thought she were just trying to protect him."

"I am certain it is true."

"If you says that's how it were, miss, I'll believe it. You're a fine lady, and a kind one, too. Anyone c'n see as *you're* not the sort to lead a man astray. Told me she loved me, she did, then run off to London."

"She suffered greatly for her foolishness."

"Why di'n't she come back home, then, arter his lordship saved her?"

"She thought you would not want her. She had nowhere to go, so his lordship took her under his protection."

"Fine words, miss, but what he done was make her his harlot, begging your pardon. I s'll knock him down agin wi' pleasure, make no doubt."

"Pray do not, Billy! He tried to persuade her to go home. She told me so herself. She chose to stay with him."

"Then what am I to do, miss?" Bewilderment succeeded anger in the poor fellow's eyes. "I wanted to make an honest woman o' her, but I won't take an unwilling wife."

Sarah wondered how to break it to him that Peggy was now willing to return, but only because Adam was leaving her. To her relief, she heard Jonathan's voice in the hall.

"The vicar is back at last," she said. "Wait here while I explain the situation to him, and then we shall see what he has to suggest."

She hurried out. Jonathan had just set his hat and gloves on the hall table. He turned at her step.

"Sarah! What is going on? You look fagged to death, my dear, and Mrs. Hicks is muttering dire predictions."

He folded her in his arms, and she clung to him wordlessly for a moment before she pulled away.

"Come into the parlour and sit down while I tell you. You must be tired, too, after driving all that way and listening to the Bishop for hours on end."

With Billy waiting in the study, she told her brother only his and Peggy's part of the story, reserving the rest of the day's happenings for later.

"So you see," she ended, "he may not be ready to marry her after all if he knows she will only have him because she cannot have Adam. And he may regard the offer of a marriage settlement as bribery, though I know it is just Adam's kindness. He said he will provide for Peggy whether she marries Billy or no. I do believe, though, that I have persuaded Billy not to attack Adam on sight."

"I shall sort it out," said her brother, unruffled. "He is in the study?"

"Yes. I think I had best come with you, for he knows me now and seems to trust me. But I shall leave before . . . Oh, Jonathan, the most difficult part." Her eyes once again fixed firmly on her hands, Sarah tried to explain what Peggy had said of the intimate relations between herself and Adam.

"My dear, you have had a difficult day!" he said sympathetically.

"You do not yet know the half of it. That will keep. Do

you think you can make Billy understand what Peggy wants?"

"Not . . . hmm, the mechanics of it, perhaps, but that he must do his best to please her. It is by no means an unreasonable expectation. I have attempted to impress it upon a number of husbands with unhappy wives, though with little success, I fear."

Sarah realized that his words confirmed Peggy's assessment of the prevailing attitude of men towards their lawful spouses. Feeling not a little indignant, she followed him to the study.

After introducing Billy to her brother, Sarah sat quietly listening to their discussion, lost in admiration of the vicar's gentle tact. He even spoke of marital relations with such matter-of-fact calm that she felt no need to leave the room. If she were ever to marry, which seemed less and less likely, she would want Jonathan to talk to her future husband just so.

She was roused from her musing when Billy stood up.

"Right, sir, I'll be off then. I'll do it just like you said. Thank you, sir, for making me see straight."

"I believe you will not regret your decision." The vicar rose and offered the groom his hand.

Billy wiped his own hand on the seat of his pants and shook the vicar's with a hearty good will, then turned and bowed clumsily to Sarah.

"Thank you, miss. I promise I won't tip his lordship a leveller next time I sees him."

Sarah nodded approvingly and he went off, looking hopeful. She turned to Jonathan.

"I wasn't listening at the end," she said. "I take it you made all right between them?"

"He means to propose, at least. I hope she will not see fit

to lead him a dance, for he must leave tomorrow to go home. His master gave him a week to settle this business."

"Is she to go with him?"

"No, he will return in a fortnight or so and stay for the reading of the banns. He seems sure of being able to persuade his master to give him leave. I told him we will take care of Peggy, but I fear it will be uncomfortable for you to have her about the house."

"I should prefer not to, I confess. Oh, I have the very thing! She shall go to Goody Newman's. The poor old woman really ought to have someone living there."

"An excellent notion. Now, tell me what else has been going on here during my absence."

Sarah glanced at the clock. "We must change for dinner at once, or it will spoil and Mrs. Hicks's dire predictions will come to pass."

Not until they settled in the parlour after dinner did she tell him about Mrs. Goudge and Marguerite. To her great surprise he was apologetic.

"My dear, I am so sorry. I'd not have had this happen for the world."

"You can hardly blame yourself, Jonathan. It is entirely Adam's doing."

"Yes, and I wish I had seen him sent to grass by that young bruiser. However, had I not encouraged him to confide in you, he'd not have directed the, ahem, ladies to the vicarage. I thought I was doing it for your own good, to open your eyes to his faults."

"You certainly succeeded in that! Pray do not worry about me, for though it was a difficult afternoon I shall not take any lasting harm, I promise you."

"I trust your resentment will not make you forget Adam's virtues, which are many. I would not have you

74

think him a monster any more than I would have you think him a saint."

"For heaven's sake let us stop talking of Adam!" said Sarah, overcome with unreasoning irritation. "Tell me what the Bishop wanted with you."

"He wants me to join the cathedral chapter." Jonathan could not hide his boyish enthusiasm. "If I accept, it is a first step towards preferment."

"You mean one day I shall be sister to the Archbishop of Canterbury? Oh, Jonathan, that is splendid. But why should you not accept?"

Her brother explained his misgivings. Life in the cathedral close would be busy, taken up with ceremonial duties and political manoeuvring, for which he had no taste, as well as ordinary parish work. He would have little time for his beloved books. He was satisfied with his peaceful existence in Little Fittleton, surrounded by people he had known all his life.

"However," he went on, "it is a great compliment, and not to be dismissed lightly. Also, it is a dull life here for you, while Salisbury has shops and assembly rooms and other amusements. I do not wish selfishly to keep you mewed up in the depths of the country. I have often regretted being unable to give you a London Season, and the minor dissipations of a cathedral town seem little enough to offer you. No, do not protest. I know you are not so frivolous as to despise country pursuits."

"I cannot imagine living anywhere else, but I should be happy anywhere with you, best of brothers. Whatever your decision, I shall not quarrel with it. When do you have to give the Bishop your answer?"

"The Church moves slowly. We have until the beginning of September. I want you to consider carefully before telling me what you would prefer to do, for I am quite unable to make up my own mind!"

They discussed the advantages and disadvantages of the move for another half hour before both began to yawn. As Sarah trudged wearily up the stairs to her chamber she realized that only one consideration was truly important to her, and she could not tell Jonathan.

If they moved to Salisbury, she might never see Adam again. But if they stayed in Little Fittleton, she would have to accustom herself to seeing him settled at Cheve House, with another woman as his wife.

Chapter Nine

≺-≺- -≻-≻

Sarah had intended, on retiring to bed, to think over the events of the day and sort out her confused emotions. She fell sound asleep within moments of lying down, and woke the next morning with nothing settled in her mind.

The first matter requiring her attention after breakfast was to send Peggy off to Goody Newman's. Billy had already departed, whistling cheerfully, but unfortunately, Sarah neglected to ensure Nellie's absence when she proposed this plan to the visitor.

"Ooh, Miss Sarah, you can't send her to that owd witch," the maid gasped in dismay.

"Peggy is no country simpleton to believe such silly talk," said Sarah firmly. "Having lived in London she is too sophisticated to heed your nonsense."

Though Peggy looked unconvinced, she was reluctant to give the lie to Miss Meade's high opinion of her. She went off with Arthur in the gig. The old woman's cottage would be a letdown after her villa in Chelsea, but it would do her no harm and in that isolated spot she was not likely ever to meet Adam.

Besides Sarah's usual chores, a number of villagers called that morning bursting with curiosity about the previous day's visitors. She managed to satisfy even the inquisitive Miss Barnes without actually revealing the truth, but leisure for contemplation was sadly lacking.

The previous day's gusty wind had dropped, and though the sky was heavy with rain clouds, Sarah decided to walk to Stonehenge. It was the only way she would find any peace, and it was warm enough not to matter if she received a wetting. She went to the kitchen to pack up some bread and cheese and fruit in a little satchel.

"Going to be a downpour any minute," prophesied Mrs. Hicks.

"The fields need rain," said Sarah tranquilly.

" 'Tes nor proper nor safe for a young lady to walk abroad alone. Suppose there be tinkers about?"

"They will be taking shelter from the downpour," she teased.

The housekeeper shook her head indulgently, used to her warnings being disregarded.

Sarah set off, walking with careful decorum through the village, then lengthening her stride when she reached the open hills. If they went to live in Salisbury, it might be impossible to escape from the town to take solitary rambles. Here everyone knew and forgave her eccentricity. Even Lady Cheverell had long since given up scolding her for it. Adam's wife would likely be more circumscribed by convention, with her position as viscountess to uphold. The proper young ladies among whom Adam was to choose doubtless would not care for such vigorous exercise in any case. After all, they were to be selected by his sisters, whose indolence, except in the ballroom, was notorious.

The sheep-cropped grass was bright with the scarlet-tinted yellow flowers of lady's slipper, a fresh reminder of the young ladies gathering at Cheve House. Doubtless, they would each bring the appropriate footwear for dancing the night away. But Sarah was shod with well-worn, sensible half boots; she was a countrywoman at heart, without the instincts necessary to the bride of a nobleman.

Not that Adam was either a dandy or an idler. She knew that even in town he rode often and exercised at Gentleman Jackson's Saloon. Could he be content with a languid, fashionable wife, or would he be driven back into the arms of the muslin company?

Sarah called herself sharply to account. She had no reason to suppose that Mary and Eliza and Louise would choose young ladies who resembled themselves. Her condemnation was motivated by jealousy of the unknown miss who would win Adam's hand. It was ridiculous to envy the girl who would have to contend with his extraordinary ability to charm every female in sight. Even if he intended to be faithful, sooner or later his scruples were bound to be overcome by his sympathy for feminine woes.

The huge grey monoliths of Stonehenge rose from the plain before her. It was said that the flat centre stone had been used for human sacrifice in the days of the Druids, but Sarah always found it a peaceful refuge. Time had laid unquiet spirits to rest, and the solitary grandeur of the place made her own concerns seem petty.

She sat down with her back against one of the stones and watched the clouds form and reform over the treeless hills. The sheep which had raised their heads on her arrival went back to nibbling at the grass. After a while she took out her luncheon. As she unwrapped the bread and cheese she was joined by a brown-and-white sheepdog which sat down at a polite distance with hopeful eyes fixed on the food. She threw a crust. The dog gulped it down, waved its shaggy tail, and trotted off about its business.

It had better manners than some humans she had met: Marguerite, for instance, who had pushed into the vicarage without a by-your-leave and as good as accused Sarah of being a lightskirt. Adam's kindness might account for his liaisons with Janet Goudge and Peggy, but the opera singer was another matter altogether. He could only have chosen to make her his mistress because he found her attractive, which seemed to indicate that his taste in women ran to the vulgar.

And if that were so, then none of his sisters' choices would suit him, for they were all bound to be the most refined, proper young ladies on the Marriage Mart.

More confused than ever, Sarah started back toward home. Really, the man was impossible! The only thing to do was to put him right out of her head and concentrate on her brother's dilemma. Would Jonathan be happier with his books and his country parish or as a rising star of the Church? There was no way she could make up his mind for him so she must do as he said and decide what sort of life she preferred.

Which brought her right back to Adam.

A few heavy drops of rain fell and she quickened her steps. She was closer to Cheve House than to the village. The soon-to-be-dowager viscountess would not mind her appearing in a shabby, and probably wet, walking dress, and she ought to ask after Jane. She felt a bit guilty about sending Adam back to town so abruptly when he had been summoned home to deal with his sister's problems.

By the time she reached Cheve, she was soaked to the skin. She slipped in at a back door and asked a surprised housemaid to inform Gossett of her arrival. Old starchy-britches (she would never be able to think of him as anything else) could be relied upon to announce her discreetly to Lady Cheverell and to send someone to find dry clothes for her.

Clad in a cast-off morning gown of Eliza's, Sarah went down to the small drawing room. Lady Cheverell was knotting a fringe in a desultory manner, while Jane stared gloomily out of the window at the pouring rain. They both brightened as Sarah entered.

"My dear, we are delighted to see you," said her ladyship, patting the sofa beside her invitingly. "Nothing is so dreary as a wet day without company."

With an affectionate smile, Sarah joined her. She was fond of Adam's mother, who always welcomed her as if she were a fifth daughter.

"I wonder that anyone chooses to go out on such a day," said Jane, taking a seat nearby. "Bradfield will not travel in the rain, I daresay. Oh, Sarah, why do you think he has not come yet?"

Sarah was taken aback by this appeal. "I fear I know nothing of the situation," she said. "Your mama told me only that you have had a disagreement with Lord Bradfield. I cannot advise you."

"Did not Adam tell you everything? I was certain he would tell you. It was not a mere disagreement. We quarrelled most dreadfully. Bradfield wants to call our child Cyril after his late papa and I threw a priceless vase at him."

"I . . . I see." Sarah did her best not to let her laughter escape her. "You are with child, then? How happy that must make you, Jane."

"Well, it would, if only . . . Oh, I see now how ridiculous it sounds." Her eyes, as blue as Adam's, swam with tears. "How very foolish I have been! I do love him, Sarah. Suppose he never comes?"

Sarah went to hug the weeping girl. She had scarce put a comforting arm about her shoulders when voices were heard in the hall. Jane clutched her.

"It is him! What shall I do? You must talk to him for me. Oh, why did Adam leave?"

Lady Cheverell was also looking at her in mute appeal. Sarah shook her head.

"No. I think it is fortunate that Adam left. It is time you stopped using a go-between and learned to settle your differences with your husband by yourself. Go on, goose, he cannot eat you. I shall come to the door with you."

She urged Jane's hesitant footsteps to the door, opened it and gave her a little push. As she closed the door she saw Jane fly across the hall and fling herself into the arms of a large, stolid-looking gentleman in a dripping multicaped greatcoat.

"Oh, Tom, I am so very sorry!" she cried.

Sarah turned to grin at Lady Cheverell, only to see her ladyship pressing a tiny wisp of lace to her eyes. It was Sarah's turn to fly across the room with an apology on her lips.

"I did not mean to upset you, ma'am. Pray tell me what is the matter?"

Lady Cheverell sniffed delicately. "You will think me such a widgeon, Sarah. It is just that you are quite right about Jane facing Bradfield without an intermissionary. I ought to have suggested it long since, but Lord Cheverell, Adam's father that is, was such a very *erasable* gentleman that I never did learn to stand up to him."

Sarah correctly translated intermissionary as intermediary, but Adam's erasable father had her at a loss for a moment. She murmured soothing words. "Oh, irascible!" she said then. "Yes, his lordship did have a notorious temper. You must not tease yourself about it, ma'am, but be thankful that whatever Adam's faults, that is not one of them."

Her ladyship looked at her guiltily. "No, he is the dearest boy," she agreed. "Only, perhaps, *too* amiable. I am so sorry, my dear, about your visitors yesterday. Every sensibility must be outraged!"

"Why, however did you learn of that? I suppose I ought to know by now that between your servants and the villagers nothing can be kept secret, but I did hope it would not come to your ears. I cannot deny that I was not best pleased by the business, but my sensibilities are shockingly impervious, I fear. I did not manage even one little swoon."

"Now you are bamming me," said Lady Cheverell with dignity. "It was very wicked of Adam. I cannot think why he would do such a disgraceful thing."

Sarah tried to explain, without further agitating her ladyship, just why Adam's Paphians had honoured the village of Little Fittleton with their disturbing presence. It was not an easy story to recount to a gently bred lady of advancing years. In the end, she blamed everything on Adam's tender heart.

"And that is my fault, too," said her ladyship tearfully when she finished. "If I had not had four daughters after Adam, he would not have grown accustomed to rescuing damsons in distress."

Sarah laughed, first at the notion that Lady Cheverell was to blame for having four girls, and then at a vision of Adam rushing about rescuing purple plums.

Lady Cheverell smiled uncomprehendingly at her mirth and went on, "All I want is for him to settle down here at Cheve with just one respectable female."

"He told us you are to have a house party to present prospective brides to him." Remembering her violent reaction to his announcement, Sarah winced.

"Yes, but I have little hope that he will find one to his

liking. Mary will bring a highly accomplished young lady who will sing and play the harp and the pianoforte, and embroider and net purses and probably even write verse. Eliza will bring a beauty, a dark beauty to act as foil to her fairness. And Louise, being the managing sort, will bring some poor, shy little creature who dare not say boo to a goose."

Sarah laughed again at this accurate summing up of the Lancing girls' preferences. "There is nothing to say that Adam will not conceive a tendre for one of them," she said.

"I cannot think it likely. I always thought he admired you excessively, Sarah. He treats you quite differently from the way he treats other females . . . at least, the ones I have seen. He certainly prefers you to his sisters."

"I believe he sees me more as a sort of brother, like Jonathan," she said bitterly. The thought flashed through her mind that Adam would never have kissed Jonathan's hand. She dismissed it. That was no more than an automatic exercise of his charm, and she did not mean to refine upon it. "We have been such good friends for so many years that it would be impossible for him to see me in a romantic light." She tried to speak cheerfully.

"Perhaps. And I daresay you would not even consider accepting his hand after his shocking behaviour. Oh dear, what a coil! I confess I should like above all things to have you for my daughter-in-law."

Before Sarah was forced to respond to this astonishing revelation, Jane danced into the room. She held up a glittering torrent of diamonds before their dazzled eyes.

"Mama, Sarah, look what Tom has brought me! That is why it took him so long to get here, because he went to London to purchase it. I told him I would sell it and buy him another Chinese vase, and he said the happiness of the mother of his heir is more important to him than any porcelain. Was not that prettily said? And the baby is to be called Thomas Cyril. Tom is gone up to take off his wet clothes. I must go to him." With rosy cheeks and eyes as bright as the diamonds, she hurried out again.

"I must go, too," said Sarah, seizing the opportunity. "I am so glad that Jane is reconciled with her husband."

"It is still raining. Do stay a little longer," urged Lady Cheverell.

"Jonathan will be wondering where I am."

"Then I shall send for the carriage. Yes, I know it is but a step to the vicarage, but two wettings in one day will never do, my dear. If you should take a chill, my house party will all come to nothing."

This mysterious utterance went unexplained, for Gossett answered the bell promptly and the bustle of departure ensued. The butler escorted Sarah down the front steps, holding a huge umbrella over her. She took her seat in Lady Cheverell's comfortable barouche, the raised hood sheltering her from the persistent drizzle.

The groom on the box was Peter, Nellie's admirer. He gave her a shy grin and saluted with his whip, then they were off. As the carriage turned down the drive, the larch grove came into view. It was dark and dripping and altogether uninviting, but Sarah remembered a bright spring day when the fresh new needles were pale green, the branches scattered with the red of developing cones.

She had been eight, to Adam's eleven. Until that day she had half resented his constant calls on her brother's time. Then came that terrifying moment when she looked down from the top of the tall larch to the ground, a dizzying distance below her, and realised that she could not climb down.

Jonathan had laughed at her. Adam, with the kindness

that was already an integral part of his nature, had climbed after her and helped her down, branch by branch, step by step.

That was the day she fell in love with him. After sixteen years of uncritical devotion, what hope had she of curing herself?

Unconsciously, she rubbed the back of her hand where his lips had touched.

Chapter Ten

<+- +>

Adam's fingers rose with a will of their own to his right cheekbone, where Sarah's fleeting kiss had landed. It was ridiculous that her casual gesture stuck in his mind.

It must be because of the contrast with the impact that had hit his left cheek shortly before, he decided. His nose was decidedly sore and a spectacular circle of purplish black surrounded his left eye. His companions were politely ignoring his appearance. He turned his attention to entertaining them.

It had proved less difficult than he expected to persuade Marguerite and Janet to share the latter's carriage. The pouring rain doubtless had helped, since it made it likely that he would stay in whichever vehicle he set out in. However, the hostility between them was almost palpable. Janet was aloof, while Marguerite chattered constantly about marquises who had complimented her singing and dukes she had danced with. By the time they stopped in Hartley Wintney for luncheon, Adam was ready to hire a hack and continue the journey on horseback even if the drizzle had continued.

Fortunately it did not. They had outpaced the rain clouds and the setting sun shone on their arrival in the city. Adam escorted his companions to their homes, promised to call on them first thing in the morning, and retreated exhausted to Mount Street.

"I trust her ladyship is well," said Gossett, eyeing his face with ill-concealed interest as he relieved him of his hat and gloves. "Your lordship will dine at home?"

"For at least a week," said the viscount sourly.

Wrigley did not let him off so lightly. The valet was appalled at the result of letting his master go off without him for a week, and said so without roundaboutation.

"Your lordship shall stay within doors for the next few days," he proposed.

This was going too far, and the viscount rounded on him with a scowl that was the more effective for being rarely seen.

"When I want you to arrange my schedule, I shall hire you as a secretary," he advised the quaking manservant. "I have two appointments tomorrow. I look to you to make me as respectable as possible."

Wrigley produced rice powder, which did somewhat soften the effect of the black eye. Regarding himself in the mirror the next morning, Adam remembered Sarah's advice to borrow Marguerite's cosmetics. He smiled and shook his head. There was tart and witty tongue hidden beneath the proper exterior of the vicar's sister.

A broad-brimmed hat shading his face, Adam set out in his closed town carriage for the Royal Exchange. Lloyd's was the obvious place to look for information on Henry Goudge's ship. If the underwriters were surprised that a nobleman looking somewhat the worse for wear was enquiring for the whereabouts of a certain India merchant, they admirably concealed it. Only their pleasure was evident when they informed him that, though reported sunk in a storm in the Bay of Biscay, the ship had only yesterday been sighted off Dungeness. With a fair wind, she would dock today, to-morrow at the latest.

Janet rose to greet Adam, her black silks rustling, hands clasped pleadingly. The incredulous joy in her face when she heard his news was ample reward for his embarrassment at Lloyd's. She sank back into her chair and he hurried to pour her a glass of wine.

"What a friend you have been to me," she cried. "I only wish I could introduce Henry to you and tell him of your kindness."

"Lord, no, not a word," said Adam nervously.

"Of course it must remain our secret, but I do hate to keep anything from Henry. Now I regret being unfaithful to him. I have been very wicked."

"Your affection for him has not wavered. Come, Janet, do not be sad. It was wrong in us, but what is past is past and cannot be mended." It was not Adam's custom to dally with married women, and he had not anticipated her sudden remorse. He blamed himself and vowed then and there never again to touch another man's wife. There were actresses and opera singers aplenty who understood these affairs and were ready to satisfy a man's needs without a second thought.

"You cannot understand," Janet was saying. "The confidence between husband and wife is one of the chief delights of marriage, and I have betrayed it. It will take me a long time to deserve his trust again, but I shall not cheat him of the joy by telling him what I have done."

"Could it not make you happier to win his forgiveness?" Adam asked, curious.

"Yes, but must I hurt him to salve my conscience? I should like to know Miss Meade's opinion. I have never met anyone like her and I admire her greatly."

"Sarah is the best of friends," he agreed. "I must be off now, or Marguerite will be wondering if I have abandoned her again. You go and put off your blacks, for Henry will expect to see you in your most cheerful array." He kissed her hand in a final farewell. It was an old-fashioned courtesy that he thought she would appreciate. Her hand was soft and white and well cared for, yet somehow it did not please him as Sarah's had. He touched his cheek, in a gesture that was becoming habitual.

"I hope you will marry a woman who has faith in you, and that you will love her enough to strive to earn her faith," said Janet solemnly.

She was becoming a veritable fount of sentimental sermons, Adam thought as he returned to his carriage and directed his coachman to stop at the first jeweller's shop in Oxford Street. Not that what she said was untrue, but he could not imagine his mother spouting such stuff, or Sarah. He made a mental note to avoid entanglements with bourgeois females in future.

The shop had precisely what he was looking for: large gems, not of the first quality, in flashy settings. Marguerite did not appreciate the restrained elegance of Rundell and Bridge's fashionable jewellery. She wanted to create a stir. He chose a gaudy bracelet of rubies arranged like blossoms with emerald leaves and diamond dewdrops. It would make a perfect farewell gift.

He stared at the shopkeeper's bill with such a look of surprise that the merchant quickly retrieved it from his hand and lowered the price by a hundred guineas. The viscount was completely unaware of the whole business. He was wondering just when he had decided to give Marguerite her congé. He signed the chit without even reading the total, thrust the velvet box into his pocket and went out to his carriage in a daze.

Conscious or not, the decision was made. That left him with the necessity of finding himself a new mistress. As the carriage turned down Poland Street, he passed in review the qualifications of all the well-known High Flyers. Most would have current protectors, of course. Though many would leave less attractive gentlemen in order to boast of having attached Lord Cheverell, Adam had no intention of arousing ill feeling.

None of the alluring faces and figures which floated across his mind's eye tempted him, and in any case he was leaving for Cheve again as soon as his face was presentable. The search could wait until he returned to town.

The carriage stopped outside the Haymarket Theatre. It was a shabby building, nearly a century old, and by daylight the gilt decoration of the interior was tawdry. According to rumour, Mr. Morris wanted to tear it down and rebuild in the modern style. Among gentlemen, the on-dit went on to explain the manager's novel plan for accumulating capital for his venture: he promised the best roles to those of his actresses with wealthy protectors who could be persuaded to pay for the privilege of seeing their lights-o'-love star upon the stage. This being understood, Adam brushed through the encounter with a minimum of unpleasantness. Mr. Morris looked complacent as he tucked into his desk drawer a bank draft for a considerable sum.

"At this rate," he admitted cheerfully, "I'll be pulling the old place down in approximately the year 1820."

"I hope you will put up a plaque with the names of your benefactors," said the viscount dryly. "Now, if you have no objection, I shall borrow your office for a private word with Marguerite."

"By all means, my lord. She's rehearsing on stage right

now. I'll call her off and give her the good news. Not more than half an hour, now." He grinned and winked.

"Ten minutes should suffice." Adam felt in his pocket for the bracelet.

"My, that's quick work!" With obvious admiration for his mistaken notion of Adam's purpose, the manager went off.

Marguerite rushed in, clad only in a number of diaphanous veils over skin-coloured tights. She flung her arms about Adam's neck and planted a smacking kiss on his sore cheek.

"Darling," she crooned. "You have made me so happy."

He extricated himself with some difficulty. "I'm glad, pet," he said. "It's by way of being goodbye, and I have . . ."

"Bloody 'ell, wotcher mean goodbye! 'Aven't I bin true ter yer all this toime? Found yerself anuvver girl, 'ave yer, so poor ol' Margrit gets left in the lurch." Hands on hips, she blazed at him, her face so red with anger that the patches of rouge were invisible.

"Be a good girl, now, pet," said Adam patiently. "I have another gift for you." He pulled the velvet case from his pocket, took out the bracelet and clasped it about her wrist.

"Cor lumme!" She held it up to the window to admire it. "That's somefing like, that is. You're a dear, Adam, and I'm sorry I kicked up a dust. I'll be sorry to lose you, and that's the truth, but all good things come to an end."

Silhouetted against the window, her charms were displayed to magnificent effect. The viscount was unmoved.

"You will find someone else in no time. With your abilities, you should hold out for a duke."

This pleased her. "So will you," she assured him, kissing his other cheek, "and the rhino's got nuffing to do wiv it. Bet I know who you've got your eye on, too. You've up and taken a fancy to that country bit, I wager."

"Sarah?" Adam's laugh was incredulous. "You are all about in your head."

"Take me for a flat? Thick as inkle-weavers, you was. 'Ave to be a discreet arrangement, what wiv 'er living at that parson's 'ouse. Won't do to flaunt her about like."

"Miss Meade is a thoroughly respectable young woman," he said angrily.

"That's how we all starts," she pointed out.

Adam stormed from the theatre in a fury. Marguerite had no idea what she was talking about, he fumed as the carriage bore him home. As if he could possibly desire his old friend Sarah, let alone have designs against her virtue!

He'd be damned if he'd ever form a liaison with an actress again. A vulgar lot they were, and appallingly temperamental into the bargain. He took out his handkerchief and scrubbed at his unhurt cheek. The doxy had probably left rouge all over him.

No more opera singers, no more lonely wives—it was beginning to look as if he should not be encouraging Peggy to marry her sweetheart. Still, he had never really been attracted by the ingenuous girl, he had just not been able to bring himself to hurt her with a rejection. Nor had he any intention of frequenting houses of ill fame. Most of their inhabitants, in his opinion, belonged in his charitable institutions.

Since he had no intention of becoming a monk, that left marriage as the only solution. His mother was right. He needed a wife.

He spent the next couple of days lurking in his house while his black eye faded. There was a certain amount of paperwork to be done for his charitable foundations, and when that palled he repaired to his library. He came across a copy of Chaucer's *Canterbury Tales,* and on a whim he looked up the description of the knight in the Prologue. Regretfully he had to acknowledge a poor fit. Generosity and courtesy he could lay claim to, and perhaps truth and honour, but as sole heir to a viscountcy with five females dependent upon it, he had not been permitted to fight in his sovereign's war. Wisdom eluded him, as he was painfully aware, and as for a maidenly modesty . . . He laughed. That, at least, Sarah would not expect of him.

He hoped she did not recall the description of the knight's son. The squire was a lover and a lusty bachelor. He had loved so hotly, apparently, that till dawn grew pale he slept as little as a nightingale. If Sarah started quoting that at him, Adam would not know where to look.

Once again decked out in rice powder and a broad-brimmed hat, he sneaked into the gallery of the House of Lords to hear Lord Lansdowne's speech. It seemed the least he could do. He managed to dodge most of his acquaintances, garnering a few peculiar looks in the process.

By the third day his eye had faded to an interesting shade of mustard yellow. Desperate for exercise, he ventured to Gentleman Jackson's saloon. Such things as black eyes were understood there, though in general the bucks of the ton avoided hitting the visible portions of each other's anatomy. A round with the Gentleman himself, a rare honour, restored the belief in his own ability which had been bruised by Billy's successful attack.

The bout finished, he wandered over to watch Lord James Kerridge sparring in a desultory manner with Mr. Frederick Swanson. He remembered that he had told his mother he would bring a couple of friends to her house party. Kerry and Swan would do very well, he thought.

Informed of this treat, Lord James demurred.

"Dash it, Adam, I ain't in the petticoat line," he objected.

"So much the better," pointed out Mr. Swanson. "It's Adam who has to find a bride. He don't want competition. Come on, Kerry, your brother ain't asked you down to the Hall till August and July in town is deuced dull. No female is going to chase you while Adam's available, so you won't have to talk to them."

Lord James allowed himself to be persuaded, and the next morning the three gentlemen rode out of London. A variety of vehicles followed at a slower pace, bearing grooms, valets, and luggage.

It was a fine day. Adam was pleased to leave the city, pleased with the company of his friends, and determined to be pleased with the eligible maidens awaiting him at Cheve. If he could not make up his mind among them, he would ask Sarah's advice.

She would laugh at him, but that was all right. He liked to hear her laugh, and to see the teasing twinkle in her grey eyes.

Chapter Eleven

✦← →✦

Sarah was rolling gingerbread dough when three large young men erupted into the kitchen.

"Sarah, I have a deal to tell you," cried Adam without ceremony, then he paused and looked round a trifle nervously. "Is Billy here?" he demanded.

"No, he went home. You are safe." She smiled at him, happy at his arrival though she wished he had not found her hot and sticky and engaged upon a domestic task. "I have a great deal to tell you, too, but will you not introduce your friends first?"

"This is Lord James Kerridge." Adam waved his hand at the tall, well-built gentleman with the slightly vacant face.

Lord James blushed crimson, bowed awkwardly, and muttered something indistinguishable.

"And this is Swan—Mr. Frederick Swanson."

Mr. Swanson was short, round, and exquisitely dressed. His face was also round, with an incongruously large nose, but his eyes held an expression of humorous intelligence.

"Delighted to make your acquaintance ma'am," he said. "You must excuse poor Kerry here. Scared to death of females."

"How unkind in you to draw attention to it," Sarah retorted, then clapped her floury hand to her mouth in dismay. "Oh, I beg your pardon, sir. We have just been introduced and I am treating you as if I had known you as long as I have known Adam." To her relief, she saw he was amused and not offended.

"Pray don't stand on ceremony, ma'am," he urged, "but I would not have you think ill of me. Kerry looks to me to make his excuses."

Lord James nodded vigorously. " 'S true," he blurted.

"I must talk to you," said Adam with some impatience, "and without these two gudgeons listening in. Take off your apron and come into the garden."

"The fire is ready," Sarah objected. "I must put the biscuits into the oven."

"Tell us what needs to be done and we'll see to it," offered Mr. Swanson gallantly. "Looks like great fun."

Lord James nodded. Sarah cast a helpless glance at Adam, who shrugged. As she hunted up a pair of clean aprons for the gentlemen, she tried to explain in a few words the art of making gingerbread men.

Adam untied her own apron, turned her round and wiped a dab of flour from her chin. "Come on," he said with a grin. "We'll make 'em eat the ones they spoil."

She followed him out.

Mr. Swanson, wielding the rolling pin with surprising skill, looked out of the window to see them wandering down the garden. Close, though not touching, they were obviously lost in their discussion.

"Smelling of April and May, the pair of them," he commented.

"Viscount Cheverell won't choose his bride from a country parsonage." Lord James shook his head for a change. "Great gun, never high in the instep, but knows what's due to his name. Lord, he's one of the biggest catches on the Marriage Mart. Imagine the kick-up if he picked a girl with no family, no fortune, and not even beauty to compensate."

"Miss Meade has a great deal of countenance, which is more important than beauty," said Mr. Swanson obstinately, but he was afraid his friend was right. As younger son of a marquis, Kerry had been brought up to such considerations.

Both of them would have been astonished if they had overheard the conversation in the garden. Two of Adam's mistresses had been quickly disposed of. Sarah was glad to hear that Henry Goudge was safe, equally glad, though surprised, that Adam had parted from Marguerite. She told him of her provision for Peggy.

"She seems to have settled down at Goody Newman's. I sent Mrs. Hicks over this morning to make sure all is going well. Billy will be back in a week or two to establish residency before the wedding."

"Shall I have to go into hiding?"

"He promised not to—hmm—'tip you a leveller' next time he sees you." She grinned at him. "Your eye is back to normal, I see."

"It was devilish embarrassing, I can tell you. I don't think Wrigley will ever let me out of his sight again. I didn't care to compromise my dignity by talking to Jem at the George on the way to town, but I spoke to him last night as we passed through, and he has agreed to marry that girl of yours."

"Nan? That is splendid! But I fear it's too late for a double wedding. I do not doubt Nan is too big by now for public display."

"Yes, they had best get hitched quietly, elsewhere. I shall see to it."

"Now, were there any other loose ends we had to tie up?"

"Jane. Mama told me you were responsible for that rapprochement. The billing and cooing is enough to turn my stomach."

Sarah laughed. "Pray do not blame me for that. All I did was refuse to help."

"As I ought to have done years ago. How wise you are!"

"I daresay a little of Jonathan's understanding may have rubbed off. He will be home any minute. I cannot think what he will say if he finds your friends in the kitchen. I must go back."

They found Jonathan, Kerry and Swan sitting round the kitchen table eating burnt gingerbread men. Sarah rushed to take the second tray of biscuits from the oven. They were done to a turn, but she gasped as she looked at them. The gentlemen had allowed their artistic talents full play. There were fish, and stars, and crescent moons, and one creature that might have been a horse, unless it was an elephant.

"I hope you don't mind, ma'am," said Lord James shyly.

"They are wonderful," she assured him. "The children will be fascinated. I cannot think why I never made anything more original than a one-legged man, and that was only because I ran out of dough."

Kerry and Swan beamed at her.

"I'd better drag them away before they eat the lot," said Adam. "Our guests will be arriving throughout the day and I promised my mother I'd be there to greet them. I shall see you later, Jon. You and Sarah are bidden to luncheon and dinner tomorrow, I collect."

"Yes," agreed the vicar. "Sarah thinks Lady Cheverell expects to need her by then to help part your squabbling sisters."

"Jonathan! You were not supposed to repeat that to Adam!" said Sarah indignantly.

"I hope they will manage forty-eight hours without a fight," Adam said, laughing, "but we shall be glad of your presence anyway."

Lord James and Mr. Swanson murmured agreement, and they left.

Sarah lay awake half that night trying to decide what to wear to Cheve House the next day. She finally settled on a round gown of smoky blue-grey muslin. It was very plain, but she knew that this year's London fashion was for the simplest, sheerest muslins and she hoped she would not look too shabby compared to the Lancing girls and their protégées. She would take with her an evening gown of amber jaconet, to change into before dinner. As she had few evening engagements, it was very little worn though it was three years old, and she had a necklace of amber beads to add a finishing touch.

Shortly after noon, Arthur hitched Dapple to the gig. It would never do to arrive at Cheve on foot on such an occasion, and besides, a fine but penetrating rain was beginning to fall. Jonathan handed Sarah in and passed her a large black umbrella. As he took the reins and joined her, she opened it, glad that there was no wind.

Despite this protection, her pelisse was damp by the time they drew up at the front door of Cheve House. A groom ran up to take charge of pony and gig, and Gossett himself welcomed them in the entrance hall.

"Her ladyship will be very glad to see you," he said in a conspiratorial voice as a footman bore off their wet coats. "She had hoped to send everyone out to walk about the grounds this afternoon."

100

"It would seem that you were not over pessimistic," Jonathan murmured to his sister, "if Lady Cheverell is already in need of leaven for her party."

Following Gossett into the large drawing room, Sarah was overcome by a momentary feeling of panic. She was not sure she could bear with equanimity the sight of Adam paying court to three beautiful and elegant young ladies. As if he guessed her thoughts, her brother laid his hand on her shoulder and gave it a gentle squeeze. She raised her chin and made her curtsy to her hostess.

Lady Cheverell did indeed look pleased to see the Meades. She drew Sarah down beside her and whispered, a mischievous sparkle in her faded blue eyes, "Only wait and see, they are just as I predicated."

Aloud, she added, "You know my girls, of course, and their husbands. And I understand you have met Lord James and Mr. Swanson."

Bows and nods and smiles and words of greeting were exchanged. Sarah responded with automatic courtesy, her eyes on the only two members of the company with whom she was unacquainted.

Beside her ladyship's eldest daughter, Louise, sat an elfin wisp of a girl in white muslin. Her pale blonde ringlets were arranged in the simplest of styles, her eyes were demurely downcast, and altogether she looked to be scarce out of the schoolroom. Louise, now Lady Edward Merriwether, introduced her as Miss Lydia Davis.

The elf rose and curtsied, gaze fixed on the floor, and murmured something in a shy little voice.

"I am happy to make your acquaintance, Miss Davis," Sarah said, while Jonathan went up to the child, bowed over her hand and seated her again.

The other stranger was at the pianoforte. Her golden

hair, very similar in shade to the Lancings', was done up in an elaborate coiffure of knots and bows. Though she was a trifle sharp-featured, her expression was lively and intelligent. She was wearing blue, but Sarah could see little of her dress because of the instrument.

Adam stood behind her, apparently having been turning the pages of her music. His second sister, Mary, presented her as Lady Catherine Carr. She did not trouble herself to rise, but bowed politely before turning to speak to Adam. He searched through a pile of sheet music, found the one she had requested, and set it on the stand. Then, to Mary's obvious chagrin, he deserted Lady Catherine to pull up a chair beside Sarah.

"What do you think?" he asked in a low voice.

"How can I possibly judge when I have barely met them?" she said with some asperity. "Where are Eliza and her beauty?"

"Mama told you her theory then." He grinned. "Eliza and her beauty, judging by last night's performance, are preparing to make their entrance."

At that moment the drawing room's double doors swung open. In the doorway, arm in arm, appeared two contrasting visions of loveliness. Eliza, the youngest of the Lancing girls, had the family's corn-gold hair, along with a startling perfection of face and figure. Her companion's ringlets were so dark as to appear black which, with her creamy complexion, suggested an Irish ancestry. Her gown, of primrose yellow almost transparent mull muslin, accentuated her dramatic colouring.

The pair posed until every eye was upon them, then moved forward in a graceful glide that Sarah knew had taken Eliza, at least, an age to perfect. Eliza's young husband, Lord Moffatt, came forward to greet her with adoration in his eyes, and the gaze she turned on him was sultry, also much practised. That honeymoon, it seemed, was not yet over.

"Miss Brennan," said Adam, "allow me to make you known to Miss Meade and her brother, who is our vicar. Sarah, Jonathan, this is Eliza's friend Miss Vanessa Brennan."

Miss Brennan swept a superb curtsy while her violet-blue eyes examined Sarah and dismissed her as competition. Sarah thought it was more habit than anything else that made the girl flutter her eyelashes at Jonathan. In a way it was flattering to have the three young ladies, the least of whom was undoubtedly an honourable, presented to her as she sat beside Lady Cheverell. On the other hand it made her feel as if she were already a dowager herself.

Adam was the next recipient of the eyelash flutter, and he followed Miss Brennan to the French doors where she pointed out something in the dripping garden. Jonathan had returned to Miss Davis's side and was endeavouring, without much success, to coax a word out of her. Sarah turned to Lady Cheverell.

"Don't tell me Adam is already conquered by Eliza's beauty," she remarked.

"Heavens, no," said his mother. "He acts just as he ought, dividing his attention equally amongst them, though he has no more success than Jonathan with little Miss Davis, I fear. Did I not tell you that Louise would bring the shyest thing in nature?"

"You did, ma'am. So far, your predictions have all proved correct. I am looking forward to a demonstration of Lady Catherine's many talents."

Lord James and Mr. Swanson were bearing down on Sarah. Just as they reached her, Gossett announced that a luncheon buffet was laid out in the dining room. Mr. Swanson gallantly requested the pleasure of escorting Sarah. Lord James, foiled, turned purple, gasped something that might have been "honoured," and offered his hostess his arm. Accepting, she beamed at him and patted his hand kindly.

Sarah refused to allow the fact that she was three inches taller than Mr. Swanson to disconcert her. It was a situation she had met with before.

"Let me show you how to do this, Miss Meade," he said with a conspiratorial grin as they entered the dining room. "I shall seat you at the far end of the table. As we pass the sideboard, you must study it and point out your favourite dishes. Then I shall dash back and fill a plate for you while everyone else is still milling about."

"I see you have your strategy well prepared, sir. If you had been in charge of provisioning the army, I daresay we should have beaten Boney years since." Sarah looked at the array of cold meats, pies, salads, pastries and fruit and remembered the trout with green peas and the mutton pasties Mrs. Hicks had served to Adam. "Heavens, I don't know where to begin! A slice of ham, I think, and one of those rolls. But how can I choose between strawberries and raspberries?"

"I shall bring you some of each," Mr. Swanson promised, "with plenty of cream."

He rushed off, and Sarah looked about at the other guests. Jonathan had brought in Miss Davis and was bending over her solicitously. Miss Brennan was looking coyly up at Adam and protesting that she never ate luncheon, it was so bad for the figure, but she would take a few cherries and a morsel of salmon in aspic, just to please him.

"*I* saw the breakfast tray she had taken up to her room,"

murmured Lord James in Sarah's ear, then turned crimson and strode off. He returned with a plate piled high with roast beef, ham and pigeon pie, which he set before Lady Cheverell. She almost disappeared behind it but smiled bravely and thanked him.

Lady Catherine was looking decidedly disgruntled. Sarah realized that she had been forced, for want of an escort, to join Mary and her husband. She recovered her countenance on being seated beside Adam. Her lively repartee soon drew the viscount's attention from Miss Brennan, who seemed to have little conversation. However, his eyes frequently strayed back to that young lady.

"Adam needs two wives," said Mr. Swanson. "The one to look at and t'other to listen to. Pity we can't somehow combine the pair of 'em."

"I expect two wives would suit him very well," Sarah answered tartly, then recollecting to whom she was speaking, she hastily changed the subject. He was right, though. Adam was laughing at something Lady Catherine had said even as his gaze slipped back to the beauty on his other side. Poor little Miss Davis had no chance against her rivals. Sarah was glad to see that the child was blossoming a little under Jonathan's kind attention.

On his way to the sideboard, Adam passed behind her chair. Stooping, he said mournfully, "No gooseberry fool," and grinned at her.

Sarah looked after him in indignation. She had missed Mrs. Hicks's gooseberry fool after accusing him of wanting to set up a harem. The wretch was roasting her.

After luncheon the party split up. Jane went to rest in her chamber, so Lord Bradfield disappeared to the billiard room with Mary's and Louise's husbands. The abandoned wives dragged their mother off to the small drawing room to tell her all about her grandchildren. Eliza and Lord Moffatt vanished to some private corner.

The rest repaired to the large drawing room. Sarah took a seat beside Miss Davis, Lady Catherine drifted to the pianoforte, and Miss Brennan adopted a languid pose on a loveseat. Lord James looked around with a hunted expression, mumbled "billiards," and turned to flee.

Adam caught him by the arm. "No you don't, Kerry," he ordered. "Go and look at Miss Brennan."

"Miss Meade?" pleaded Kerry. "Conversable female, Miss Meade."

"Miss Brennan. You don't have to talk to her, just look at her."

Sarah, who had overheard every word, caught Adam's eye. She had to concentrate very hard to keep from laughing.

Adam stayed talking to Jonathan, while Mr. Swanson did his duty by joining Lady Catherine. Sarah turned to Miss Davis.

"Do you live near Louise?" she enquired.

"Yes, ma'am. Lady Edward has been very good to me." The soft voice was dubious.

"Perhaps you feel a little strange so far from home with no relative to support you?"

"I am not much used to company, and I do not know very well how to go on."

"I thought you must have had your Season in London already."

"Oh no!" Miss Davis's brown eyes filled with horror at the thought. "I mean, though I am eighteen, Papa does not care for London society, and anyway, Mama is too busy with the children to take me."

"You have many brothers and sisters?"

Sarah was treated to an enthusiastic description of a horde of small half brothers and sisters, for "Mama," it seemed, was Miss Davis's stepmother. "Papa," Baron Davis of Clwyd, was more interested in his horses and hounds than in finding a husband for his eldest daughter. Both had been delighted by Lady Edward's invitation to Cheve House.

Lydia—Miss Davis begged Sarah to call her thus and shyly agreed to reciprocate—not only missed the children but feared that the younger ones might forget their letters during her absence. Sarah told her about the school she meant to start.

"What a splendid idea! How I should like to do something like that."

"Adam means to support it financially. He is the most generous of gentlemen."

"You have known Lord Cheverell forever, have you not? He is very handsome and dashing. I am sure he thinks me a complete ninnyhammer, for I have not the least notion what to say to him. Your brother is much easier to talk to."

"It is Jonathan's business to be easy to talk to. Do not be afraid of Adam, I beg of you. He is as kind as Jonathan in his way."

"I shall try not to be," said Lydia obediently.

Adam came up to them at that moment, it being Miss Davis's turn for her share of his attention. Sarah mentioned that the girl was teaching her siblings to read and he took the hint. As she went to listen to Lady Catherine's performance of a Scarlatti sonata, she had the satisfaction of leaving Lydia happily chatting about his lordship's orphanages.

It was a hollow satisfaction.

Chapter Twelve

Following a formal dinner, the evening was spent at cards and word games. Lady Catherine excelled at the latter, producing clever verses on any subject at a moment's notice, which was certainly why Mary had insisted on playing that particular game. Adam was amused, but Sarah doubted that a talent for rhyme was what he looked for in a wife.

When the tea tray was brought in, Jonathan asked for the gig to be brought round in half an hour. He and Sarah made their farewells, and Lady Cheverell assured them that she would bring most if not all of the party to church the next morning.

"Mary has planned a musical evening on Monday," she went on. "I do hope you will come, for if it is nothing but Couperin and Haydn I shall fall asleep."

Adam escorted them into the hall, where they found Wrigley hovering, apparently concealing something behind his back.

"My lord?" the valet said diffidently. "I believe your lordship has forgotten . . ."

"Oh yes, thank you, Wrigley." The viscount took the small package wrapped in brown paper tied with string. "Sarah, I brought you a little present from London. Don't open it till you get home, but be careful, it is breakable."

Flustered, Sarah accepted the gift and expressed somewhat confused gratitude. He had never given her anything before, or at least, not since her tenth birthday. She still had the crooked wooden horse he had carved for her on that momentous occasion. Wondering what was in the package, hoping that the contents would enlighten her as to Adam's motive in giving it, she answered at random Jonathan's comments on their visit as he drove back to the vicarage.

Taking her candle from the hall table, she hurried up to her chamber. She sat down at her dressing table and set the package beside the candle, with a sudden curious unwillingness to discover what it contained. If it was fragile, it could not be jewellery. Of course Adam's sense of propriety, though flexible, would not permit a gift of jewellery to a lady to whom he was not related. Too wide and short for a fan. Surely not a porcelain figurine: he knew her lack of interest in frivolous ornaments which had to be dusted.

She took it up and weighed it in her hand. It was quite heavy for its size. Laughing at herself for dallying, she untied the string, and unwrapped a cut-glass bottle.

Lotion of the Ladies of Denmark. Sarah had heard of it, a fashionable preparation for preventing wrinkles and softening rough skin. Her lips trembling, she studied her face in the glass. It was browner than it ought to be, but there was no trace of a wrinkle that she could find. Why had Adam given it to her?

Then she recalled his final gesture before he left for London. He had kissed her hand. She had treasured the moment, aware of her own foolishness but never guessing that all he remembered of it was her work-roughened skin. A single tear ran down her cheek. She brushed it away angrily, eased the stopper from the bottle and poured a little of the lotion into the palm of her hand.

It had an agreeable fragrance. Slowly she massaged it

into her skin. Adam was incapable of intentional cruelty; therefore he had meant the gift to give her pleasure. She would thank him for it, tease him a little about trying to make her over into a lady of fashion.

At least he had thought of her when he was in town.

By some miracle, Lady Cheverell brought her entire party to morning service the next day. The village and farm folk gaped as the elegant visitors strolled into the little church. The Cheverell pew was far too small to hold everyone, so Adam brought Miss Davis to join Sarah in the vicarage pew. He was followed by a determined Miss Brennan, dressed quite unsuitably for church in another sheer muslin with ribbons the colour of her eyes. Mr. Swanson accompanied her.

Lord James, looking uncomfortable as always, seated Lady Catherine beside Mary and her husband and then fled to join his friends. With dogged determination, he stumbled over everyone's feet until he reached Sarah. She moved to allow him space to sit, which he sank into with a sigh of relief, wiping his forehead.

Sarah handed him a prayer book and a hymn book. His look of alarm warned her that it had been some time since he had been to church. So she took the books away and shared hers with him, nudging him at intervals throughout the service when it was time to kneel or stand.

Jonathan preached a sermon on the text, "The labourer is worthy of his hire," to which Lord James listened with flattering attention.

"Devilish good speech," he assured Sarah in a whisper at the end, with such evident intention to please that she did her best to hide her amusement. She smiled with what she hoped looked like gratitude for his appreciation, while relishing in advance the moment when she could repeat his praise to her brother.

After the service, they emerged from the church to find that the sun had come out. It was Miss Brennan's turn for Adam's escort. Sarah thought she saw a gleam of gratification in the young beauty's violet eyes when she realized that most of the local people were waiting in the churchyard. To be seen on the viscount's arm in such a situation could only enhance her chances, and she smiled and nodded with the utmost graciousness when he paused to exchange a word here and there. Sarah caught a few shocked comments on Miss Brennan's gown, but they were far outweighed by approving wonder at her loveliness.

Lady Catherine looked furious and stonily ignored the populace.

"Shocking bad tactics," murmured Mr. Swanson.

Lydia, at his side, shot him a frightened glance.

"He is not castigating you, my dear," Sarah reassured her. "Why do you not go and point out to Lady Catherine the mistake she is making, sir? You will know how to be tactful about it. Lord James will take care of Miss Davis, will you not, my lord?"

Lord James managed a strangled assent and Mr. Swanson went off on his errand of mercy. Sarah saw Lady Catherine scowl at him, but she then took his arm and gracefully acknowledged the villagers' bows and smiles.

"I must be on my way," Sarah told her companions. "Jonathan has to preach in the next village this afternoon, and I must see that he eats before he leaves."

Lord James and Miss Davis regarded each other with mutual terror and turned pleading eyes to her. Fortunately, for Sarah really was in a hurry, Louise came up at that moment to take charge of her protégée, rushing her off after

Adam. Lord James Kerridge might be the son of a marquis, but he was only a younger son, and a mooncalf at that.

The mooncalf turned a reproachful look on Sarah. "Gave me quite a turn there. I say, like to call this after-noon. With your permission. Don't mind sitting in the kitchen."

"Oh, I think we might allow you in the parlour," she said, smiling. "But Jonathan will not be there, so pray do not come alone."

"Bring a chaperone," he promised, returning her smile.

He was very good-looking when he smiled, the vacant look vanishing. Sarah suspected that in male company he was perfectly compos mentis. She wondered what had caused his timidity with the female sex. It was flattering that he felt confident enough with her to actually seek her out.

He brought not one chaperone but three. Sarah was sitting on a shady bench in the garden, reading, when she heard the sound of hooves. Round the corner of the coach house came four horses. Adam waved to her from Caesar's back, dismounted, and lifted Lydia down from a pretty mare. The other two riders were Lord James and Mr. Swanson.

The exercise had brought a hint of rose to Lydia's cheeks and she looked charming in her brown velvet riding habit. Tying the horses, Adam gazed after her with approval as she tripped down the path towards Sarah.

"Miss Meade, I hope you will not think me forward for coming uninvited."

"On the contrary, I think you backward, for you promised to call me Sarah, remember? I am delighted to see you. Sit here beside me, and we shall make the gentlemen stand. It is a beautiful day for a ride."

"Do you ride, Miss Meade?" Mr. Swanson enquired,

coming up in time to hear her comment.

"Rarely. Our pony, Dapple, is not quite the right shape for a lady's mount."

Adam shouted with laughter, then suddenly grew serious, almost angry. "You know perfectly well that you are welcome to take any hack you like from the Cheve stables," he said. "They eat their heads off waiting for my sisters' visits."

"Come down off your high ropes, Adam. I have never been accustomed to riding regularly and I am perfectly happy to walk or drive, I assure you. But what of Lady Catherine and Miss Brennan? How is it that they do not accompany you?"

Not completely pacified by Sarah's words, Adam turned his irritation in a new direction. "As it happens they were otherwise occupied and I for one do not regret it. Lady Catherine is so determined to demonstrate her superior horsemanship that she is bound to come to grief sooner or later. I've no desire to be present when it happens. And Miss Brennan only ventures on horseback so that we may admire her form in an equestrian pose. She will not go above a walk, which is devilish dull."

"Ladies present, old chap," Mr. Swanson reminded him.

"Oh, Sarah don't mind what I say." The viscount recollected himself. "Beg pardon, Miss Davis. I let my tongue run away with me, I fear. You, at least, ride simply because you enjoy riding."

Lydia blushed and studied her gloves with apparent fascination. Sarah was glad that the girl had at last scored a point against her rivals, though it was a great pity that she was still tongue-tied in Adam's presence. She was an engaging child, once one had broken through the barrier of her shyness.

Sarah invited her guests to go up to the house to take refreshments. She and Adam led the way.

"As a matter of fact," he said in a low voice, "what I told you was only half the truth. Lady Catherine and Miss Brennan seem to feel it beneath their dignity to call at the vicarage. No doubt Mary and Eliza will soon set them right, for my sisters must surely be aware that I have not the slightest intention of marrying any toplofty miss who will not acknowledge you as a friend."

Once again his intended kindness hurt her to the core. She fought past the lump in her throat to say with tolerable composure, "You must not let that condition stand in your way, for perhaps Jonathan will accept the post in Salisbury. If we remove from here, it will not matter what your wife thinks of us."

He frowned. "He mentioned the possibility to me, but I thought him inclined against the move. Living at Cheve year-round would be intolerable without you and Jonathan in the village."

"Then you had best choose a wife who will be as happy in town as in the country." It was a relief to reach the house. Sarah asked Mrs. Hicks to bring tea to the parlour and they all adjourned thither.

Conversation turned to the ball which Lady Cheverell had planned for the centrepiece of her house party. Sarah and Jane had written the invitations for her while Adam was in London and they had been sent out to all the neighbouring gentry.

"Louise has taken charge of the decorations," Adam said. "She is going to deck the walls with larch boughs, I understand. She described it as a 'sylvan bower.' Do you remember the masquerade ball she insisted on in her coming out year, Sarah? You were too young to attend, but I paraded before you in my Cavalier costume."

"I remember all too well," she responded dryly. "Jonathan dressed as a Roundhead and the two of you started a mock sword-fight in the middle of the ballroom. It was the talk of the county for months, and your mother has refused to hold a masquerade since."

"I'm sure I don't know why. Everyone would come in hope of a repeat performance."

"Everyone comes to Lady Cheverell's balls anyway. She tells me she has had nothing but acceptances, even from Lord and Lady Lansdowne, though Bowood is quite twenty miles off."

"The Marquis of Lansdowne is a political associate of mine," said Adam in a lofty voice.

Sarah, Mr. Swanson and Lord James all laughed heartily.

"It's true! Dash it, I even sneaked into the Lords with a black eye to listen to his antislavery speech."

Lydia looked shocked. Whether it was by his lordship's black eye or by his political affiliation with a reformist Whig, no one bothered to ask.

"And I thought your excuse to your mother was sheer prevarication," Sarah mocked. "She told me you claimed that speech as your reason for fleeing—I beg your pardon—hurrying to town."

Mr. Swanson appeared to be on the point of demanding an explanation for this interesting exchange, but Mrs. Hicks entered with the tea tray just in time to save Adam from interrogation.

The next afternoon bore out Adam's faith in his sisters. The vicarage received a visit from Louise and Mary, accompanied by Lydia, Lady Catherine and Miss Brennan.

Sarah had never been on intimate terms with the Lancing girls, but long acquaintance made chatting with them second nature. The other three guests were less easy to entertain. Lydia proved as silent in feminine company as she was in masculine. Lady Catherine looked disparagingly about the parlour and commented on the lack of space for a pianoforte. Miss Brennan, with no gentleman present to admire her, sulked until the talk turned to fashion, and then attempted to monopolize the conversation. In this she had little success; she was Eliza's friend and both Louise and Mary had considerable expertise in the art of quashing younger sisters.

Mary also managed to put Lady Catherine in a position where she was forced to make Sarah free with her Christian name. Gravely returning the privilege, Sarah hid a smile. When she and Lydia had greeted each other informally, Louise had looked smug. It seemed Mary was afraid her sister had taken a point in the battle for Adam's favour.

Miss Brennan's mentor was not present to urge her to follow suit, but the daughter of an Irish viscount could hardly hold back when the daughter of an English earl led the way. In no time Sarah found herself with the doubtful felicity of being on first-name terms with all of Adam's prospective brides.

Vanessa (lately Miss Brennan) and Lydia both brightened visibly when Jonathan came in from a parish visit. After their guests had left, Sarah laughingly teased her brother about this.

"I believe Miss Brennan would welcome a carter's lad if there were no other male present to minister to her vanity," he answered with a grin. "Even a humble vicar is grist for her mill when no more worthy gentleman is about."

"She is very like Eliza, is she not? Her looks fill her mind to the exclusion of all else. However, Eliza seems sincerely attached to her Lord Moffatt, so perhaps Vanessa will learn to appreciate Adam properly if he chooses her. Lydia is another matter, though. She talked to Adam quite happily about his orphanages, yet on other subjects she is dumb. With you she is more comfortable even than with me."

"If a vicar cannot put a shy child at ease, he is not worthy of his cure. She is an unsophisticated innocent, but there is enough kindness in Adam to win her over in time."

"If he should choose to. I begin to think it somewhat unfair of Lady Cheverell to confront him with this situation."

After dinner, the Meades drove to Cheve House for the musical evening. A new guest was present, Lady Cheverell's brother, Sir Reginald Makepeace. An intimate of the Prince Regent, he was a rotund gentleman, an inveterate gossip with an endless fund of amusing anecdotes. Sarah liked him and went willingly to join him when he beckoned to her.

"What a welcome, eh, missy?" he grumbled. "If I'd known what m'sister had in store for this evening, I'd have arrived tomorrow."

"Of course you are used to the finest professional musicians, sir. Our amateur efforts cannot compare."

" 'Tis true Prinny always hires the best for his musical entertainments. However, I am not above being pleased and I seem to recall a ditty you and your brother and m'nephew performed some years since."

"It is hardly fitting for such elegant company, sir, but if it will amuse you to hear it again, I daresay I can persuade them."

"Do that. You're a sensible woman, m'dear." He beamed at her with far more fondness than he had ever displayed for any of his nieces.

Since Mary had had a hand in arranging the evening, inevitably Lady Catherine was the chief performer. Mary's harp had been unearthed from some lumber room and refurbished, and her protégée played several pieces upon this and upon the pianoforte. Her performance was polished, even brilliant at times, but Sarah thought it lacking in any deeper feeling.

She was castigating herself as an old cat when Sir Reginald leaned towards her and observed, "All surface show. That's enough of that. Time to put the rest through their paces." He raised his voice. "Miss Brennan, will you not favour us with a tune?"

Lady Catherine cast him a look of dislike but gave up her seat. Miss Brennan glided forward in her inimitable style. Her pose at the piano displayed her figure to advantage, distracting the attention of the gentlemen, at least, from her wooden performance. She sang a romantic ballad to her own accompaniment, but the work of art was her curtsy afterwards.

"Miss Meade's turn," said Sir Reginald promptly, before Miss Brennan could begin another song.

"Oh yes," seconded Lady Cheverell. "Will you and Jonathan do that lovely duo from *Orpheus and Euripides*? I have not heard it in years."

"Nor have we sung it in years, ma'am," Sarah admitted wryly, "but if Mary will accompany us as she used to we will attempt it."

Gluck's music was unforgettable, and where Sarah forgot the words she filled in with syllables she hoped sounded Italian. Jonathan performed his part with aplomb.

"Well done, Orpheus," she said from the corner of her mouth as they acknowledged the polite clapping.

"Well done, yourself, Eurydice, or should I say Euripides?"

"Lady Cheverell's malapropisms are a constant delight, are they not? Sir Reginald wants to hear 'Widecombe Fair.' Shall we oblige?"

"By all means. Adam, we need your talents!" After a minor argument about the order of the names in the chorus, they embarked upon the adventures of Bill Brewer, Jan Stewer, Peter Gurney, Peter Davy, Dan'l Whidden, 'Arry 'Awke, old Uncle Tom Cobbleigh and all. As always, Adam's version of a Devonshire accent was the highlight of the folk song. Halfway through the audience began to join in, with much confusion, and they ended to tumultuous applause.

Sir Reginald winked at Sarah. "Livened it up a bit, eh?" he said.

The uproar died down and Louise took charge. "Lydia will sing to us now," she proclaimed. "Come, my dear, there is no need to be afraid. The Mozart, I think, and I shall play for you."

"What the deuce is m'niece up to?" wondered Sir Reginald as an unwilling Lydia was coaxed and bullied into compliance. "She looks like the cat that stole the cream."

Lydia's voice was tremulous at first, but after a few bars she lost her self-consciousness and her clear, true soprano rang through the room. Even Louise's enthusiastic but erratic accompaniment could not detract from the glory of the sound. The aria ended in a breathless hush, succeeded by a clamour of approval. Crimson-cheeked, Lydia fled from the room.

"She is not used to any audience but her family," explained Louise with a triumphant smile. "I shall go after her."

Sarah caught Jonathan's eye and a glance of comprehension passed between them. He intercepted Louise on her way out of the drawing room, and Sarah knew he was persuading her not to drag poor Lydia back to face the congratulations.

Adam wandered over to Sarah's side. "One in the eye for Mary," he observed. "Little Miss Davis cast even her prodigy into the shade and made the rest of us look nohow."

"That's shockingly ungallant of you, nevvy," reproved his uncle.

"Oh, I can say anything to Sarah. She will not take offense."

If he says that one more time, thought Sarah, *I shall scream.*

Chapter Thirteen

<+- -+>

Though Sarah had been too young for Louise's masquerade, she had since attended many balls at Cheve. She had always enjoyed them, never having suffered the ignominy of being a wallflower. In fact, it was on those occasions that she had met the gentlemen who subsequently offered for her hand, only to be refused. How could she accept Sir Martin Waytsley or Mr. Gervaise Riggs when she remembered all too clearly her last dance with Adam?

She was not looking forward to the coming ball, and she was not sure why. There was no reason to suppose she would lack for partners. Jonathan had reserved the first dance; Mr. Swanson and Lord James Kerridge had already begged her to save them each a set; Lady Cheverell's sons-in-law might be relied upon for a few more; and the gentlemen of the local gentry were unlikely suddenly to decide to ignore her. To be sure, with three young ladies to court, Adam might not have time to stand up with her, but that was a poor reason for her reluctance to attend. Nonetheless, she was reluctant.

"I believe I shall claim a headache on Saturday," she said impulsively to Jonathan at breakfast on Thursday.

In his surprise he swallowed a morsel of toast the wrong way and choked. As soon as pats on the back and a mouthful of tea allowed, he gasped out, "Why on earth would you do such a nonsensical thing?"

"I am quite on the shelf by now and it is unbecoming in an old maid to put herself forward."

"Fustian! Even if you were so prim and proper as to believe that, it is not true that you are on the shelf, my dear. Only look at the way Swan and Kerry follow you about."

"What has that to say to anything? According to Adam they are both confirmed bachelors. Besides, I have nothing to wear."

"So now we come to the crux of the matter." Jonathan laughed. "Go into Salisbury and buy yourself a new ball gown. I suppose it is too late to have one made up in time, but surely you can find something suitable and have it altered."

"The new styles are so simple that I daresay it would be possible," admitted Sarah grudgingly.

He gave her no chance to raise further objections. Dapple was hitched to the gig and Sarah drove off with Mrs. Hicks beside her, delighted at the rare opportunity to visit the superior shops of Salisbury.

When they returned, some eight hours later, the gig was full of packages. Most were of a prosaic domestic nature, but one bore the name of Salisbury's premiere modiste and contained, swathed in tissue paper, a delightful confection of gold net over white satin. No one could have guessed that the rouleau around the hem had been rapidly added by expert fingers to allow for Miss Meade's slender height. The white satin corsage, embroidered with gold thread, was somewhat lower than Sarah was accustomed to. She consoled herself with the certainty that Vanessa's and Eliza's necklines would be lower still.

The gown had not been cheap. After spending so much

money, she was committed to going to the ball.

During her absence, Adam, Swan and Kerry had called, ostensibly to deliver an invitation to dinner that evening. The three gentlemen spent a part of every day at the vicarage, sometimes accompanied by other members of the party. Since she and Jonathan were invited daily to Cheve House, Sarah had ample opportunity to observe Adam's behaviour toward Lydia, Catherine and Vanessa. As far as she could tell, he treated them with absolute impartiality. Lady Catherine amused him, he enjoyed looking at Vanessa, and he was patiently gentle with Lydia. If he had any preference, he did not show it.

Swan suggested a reason for this when he said, "It's my belief he don't care to let one of his sisters lord it over t'others while he's stuck in the same house!"

Sarah found it painful to watch Adam doing the pretty to three eligible young ladies. She frequently reminded herself that she had never had any real hope of him seeing her in a romantic light. It was ridiculous to dread the ball.

She devoted considerable thought to the matter and at last worked out why this ball was different from the many she had enjoyed. Adam used to be the unreachable god. She had been grateful for the least sign of attention from him. Now he was revealed to her as a human being with human failings. As such, he was in theory more accessible to her, yet in practice she had no greater expectations from him than she had ever had.

She tried to be satisfied with his friendship.

The evening of the ball arrived. Sarah put on her new gown and examined her reflection in the looking glass on her dresser. It was impossible to see herself from head to toe at one time, but by tilting the mirror she studied herself bit by bit, starting at the bottom.

Her white silk dancing slippers were veterans, but Mrs. Hicks had refurbished them so that the wear scarcely showed. Nellie had carefully pressed the skirts of the new gown and there was not a wrinkle to be seen. The neckline was lower than she had thought. She tugged at it nervously, then put on her gold locket with the miniatures of her parents. That would distract attention from the alarming expanse of bosom visible above the brief bodice.

Her face—well, there was nothing to be done about that. Her coiffure, all wrong for the frivolous dress, was another matter.

She opened her chamber door and called, "Mrs. Hicks!"

The housekeeper hurried up the stairs, followed by Nellie, and they all crowded into the little room.

"Oh miss, if you en't pretty as a picture!" marvelled the maid.

Between them, they succeeded in fastening her hair in a knot on the crown of her head, from which loose ringlets fell to her shoulders. It felt a bit unstable, but Sarah was pleased with the effect. She took up her gloves and the gold net reticule she had extravagantly purchased to match the gown, and went down to the parlour.

Jonathan was waiting, handsome in his black coat and black silk knee breeches.

"Beautiful," he exclaimed. "I hope you are ready to leave or we shall be late to dinner."

To Sarah's relief he did not comment on her décolletage. By the time Gossett ushered them into the drawing room at Cheve, she had forgotten it, secure in the knowledge that her brother would not let her make a cake of herself. She paused in the doorway as the butler announced their arrival.

Adam was talking to a distinguished-looking gentleman

in his mid-thirties. They both glanced towards the door as the Meades' names were pronounced. An expression of startled admiration crossed Adam's face as he saw Sarah. He said something to his companion, who answered with a nod and followed him across the room.

Adam's blue eyes were warm as he took Sarah's hand and bowed over it. "Miss Meade, Lord Lansdowne has asked to be presented to you, but before I allow him that privilege I mean to secure my own position. May I request the honour of the supper dance?"

"I shall be delighted, my lord." Her voice was prim but her eyes glinted with amusement at his formality.

Once introductions were concluded, the marquis stood talking to Jonathan for a few minutes, while Adam drew Sarah aside.

"Gold becomes you," he said. "You should wear it more often."

"Can you picture me in the kitchen making gingerbread all bedecked in gold?"

He smiled. "Perhaps it would be impractical. After all, the gold in your eyes should be enough for any man."

The depth of sincerity in his voice took Sarah's breath away; she could not think how to answer. Then Lord Lansdowne interrupted.

"Do you not agree, Cheverell? Oh, I beg your pardon, I see your mind is on beauty, not politics, this evening. Miss Meade, allow me to steal you from your admirer for a moment. I should like to make you known to my wife."

Sarah found the marchioness a friendly, unpretentious young woman and remained by her side until dinner was announced. As the highest ranking lady present, Lady Lansdowne was taken in by Adam, while her husband escorted Lady Cheverell. Sarah was pleased to find herself seated between Mr. Swanson and the squire of the next village, an old friend.

Jonathan was sitting opposite her, with Miss Davis at his side. Lydia was dressed in white crape embroidered with silver thread, a silver fillet in her fair hair. As she chatted with the vicar, her ethereal loveliness was enhanced by the unwonted animation of her expression.

Laughing at one of Swan's witty comments, Sarah glanced round the table to see what Vanessa and Catherine were wearing, for she had not noticed them in the drawing room. Lady Catherine was in her favourite blue, with a multitude of ribbons and knots and bows. Vanessa's gown was an unusual shade of pale lilac, calculated to bring out the colour of her eyes. Sarah had not consciously chosen her dress with the same end in view, but she wondered now whether Adam might suspect her of having done so. Had he been teasing her with his pointed reference to the gold in her eyes?

After dinner, more guests began arriving, and soon the musicians struck up the opening cotillion in the larch-bedecked ballroom. Adam again partnered Lady Lansdowne.

Leading Sarah into the set, Jonathan commented, "Wise man. He does not want to raise the hopes of any of the three by any distinguishing attention. The first dance is practically a declaration."

"So that is why you chose to stand up with me," said Sarah, her rallying tone concealing her chagrin, "and why Adam asked me to take supper with him." He looked at her with sympathetic understanding but did not contradict her. Mr. Swanson confirmed her suspicion when she took to the floor with him for the second dance.

"Poor Adam had the deuce of a time trying to decide in what order to take his three damsels without either encouraging or disappointing them. In the end he settled on strict formal precedence: Lady Catherine, Miss Brennan and then Miss Davis, whose papa is a mere baron. Lady Edward is most displeased."

"Because she is his eldest sister and her protégée is last on the list?" Sarah managed to laugh.

The last vestige of her joy in Adam's compliment vanished when she overheard him telling Vanessa that her eyes reminded him of violets drenched in dew.

Beside that extravagant description, his simple words to Sarah seemed commonplace.

The supper dance was a country dance. Sarah was glad that the figures often separated her from Adam, for she was afraid he might guess her hurt. When they came together, he was noticeably ill at ease and their usual comfortable camaraderie was missing.

All too soon the orchestra played the final cadence, set down their instruments and straggled from the ballroom in search of refreshment. The guests followed suit, in the opposite direction. Adam and Sarah made their way toward the supper room.

"I noticed you stood up with Lord Lansdowne," he said, carefully casual.

"He is a good dancer and a fascinating conversationalist." Her words sounded stilted to her own ears. "Lady Lansdowne, too, is charming."

"I am glad you like them. I mean to do more in Parliament in future, and he will sponsor me. It is all very well founding charities, but they can touch so few people. The government must be moved to act in favour of the unfortunate on a large scale. But this is no topic for a ballroom. Sit here, and I shall bring you something to eat."

He had led her to a table for two in a comparatively

quiet corner. By the time he returned, she had composed her mind and was determined to behave with her normal cheerfulness. She was no child, to allow a passing disappointment to spoil the entire evening.

He, too, was more like his usual self. "I brought you some chicken and mushroom vol-au-vents," he announced. "I remember you making a pig of yourself on them the first time you came to a ball at Cheve." He poured champagne from the bottle on the table.

"I remember," she agreed reminiscently. "That was the time you ate too much syllabub and Jonathan had to hurry you into the garden before you disgraced yourself."

"There are some aspects of the past that are better forgotten. Here's to the future." He raised his glass to her and she sipped from her own.

Their eyes met over the sparkling liquid and she lowered hers in confusion at the seriousness in his.

"Dash it!" Glancing round the noisy room, Adam ran his fingers through his hair, ruining the effect Wrigley had struggled to achieve. His forelock flopped back over his forehead. "There are too many people here by half."

"Surely there are not above a hundred." Sarah chose to return the conversation to polite normalcy. "Your mama was happy to have so many accept, though London hostesses often invite several hundred, I collect."

"They do, and I do not mean to boast, but I have had as many as a dozen caps set at me in a single evening, so why should a mere three put me out of temper?" Adam grinned at her.

"You are too high in your own conceit. Lydia is by no means setting her cap at you. On the other hand, Miss Susan Fielding and Lady Amalthea Trent are both pouting because you have not asked them to stand up with you."

"I cannot dance with everyone. My sisters will have three fits if I do not give their favourites two apiece. What do you think of them, by the way?"

"The three favourites?" Tempted to tear three reputations to shreds, Sarah hunted for something complimentary to say of each. "Lady Catherine astonishes me with the breadth of her accomplishments. Her musical performance is superior, her sketching admirable and her conversation witty. I have often heard you laughing at the stories she tells of your London acquaintance."

"She has a talent for making an on-dit amusing, to be sure, but her wit is not infrequently malicious."

"Well then, Vanessa: she is quite the most beautiful creature I have ever seen, always excepting Eliza, of course."

"Eliza is quite the silliest of my sisters, and her friend takes after her. For all her speaking looks, Miss Brennan has not a sensible word to say for herself."

"You are harsh. At least Lydia is kind enough and intelligent enough to take an interest in your orphanages. She is interested in education and adores children, I understand."

"I mean to set up my nursery, not to spend my days in it, and as a sole topic of conversation, it will quickly pall."

"Heavens, Adam, you are excessively hard to please. Do you feel no slight preference for any of them?"

"Miss Davis is the best of the bunch, I suppose. However, I've no intention . . . Mama?"

Lady Cheverell came up to their table. "The orchestra is returning to the ballroom, dearest. If you and Sarah were to make a move in that direction, the rest will go, too. Whatever have you done to your hair, Adam? Let me smooth it down."

Adam sat patiently while his mother patted at his head,

finishing with an unsuccessful attempt to persuade the errant lock to stay back.

"Thank you, Mama." He stood up and kissed her cheek. Offering his arm to Sarah, he proceeded toward the door of the supper room.

There was an immediate move to follow.

" 'All we, like sheep . . .' " quoted Sarah.

He looked down at her and laughed. Their inexplicable awkwardness with each other had passed, but she could not help wondering what he had been going to say.

Chapter Fourteen

Adam was in love.

But he was not ready to admit it, even to himself. He only knew that his feelings for Sarah had changed irrevocably in that moment when he looked up and saw her regal figure standing in the doorway. For the first time, he had seen her as a woman, not just as a companion of his childhood and the best of friends.

Busy about the duties of a host, he had not had time to consider the revelation or its consequences. When at last his turn came to dance with her, he had been unable to treat her with his usual teasing informality, yet he had not known what should be in its place. As if sensing his uncertainty, she had been distant. The constant parting and rejoining of the dance had frustrated his need to break through the sudden barrier between them.

And then, when he was able to speak to her properly, he had started on a serious subject on which they were in complete sympathy, only to realize that this was neither the time nor the place.

Not until they returned to the ballroom did he feel at ease with her again, and he found himself back on the old, friendly footing. It was comfortable, but it was not what he wanted.

His first partner after supper was Miss Davis. Not once

in the course of the dance did she interrupt his thoughts by addressing a remark to him, for which he was duly grateful. He left her with Louise and went to look for Miss Brennan. She was standing by the open French doors onto the terrace, fanning herself and whispering with Eliza.

"Adam, it is unbearably stuffy in here, and poor Vanessa is feeling a little faint," his youngest sister informed him. "I promised her you would take her out onto the terrace."

It was a warm, moonlit night, and several couples were visible taking the air, strolling about or leaning against the stone balustrade. Miss Brennan looked her usual imperviously beautiful self, neither flushed nor pale, but Adam could scarcely accuse her of deceit. He succumbed to good manners and escorted her outside.

"That is a little better," she murmured, with a sigh designed expressly to draw attention to her exquisite bosom.

She let go Adam's arm and drifted down the shallow steps to the garden. He followed perforce.

"Miss Brennan, I believe we ought to return to the ballroom," he protested. "There is a chill in the air and it will never do for you to catch cold."

"I shall be warm enough if we walk a little. Do let us go just so far as the jasmine bower. Its fragrance is so sweet at night. It will revive me."

She seemed in little need of reviving, for she took his arm again and walked determinedly away from the house. Soon they were beyond the reach of the lights in the ballroom, their way illuminated only by the moon.

Then Miss Brennan tripped.

Adam reached to save her from falling. Somehow, she was in his arms, pressed full-length against his body, her face raised to his. Instinct won out and he bent his head to drop a kiss on her rosebud lips.

He came to his senses immediately but her arms were around his neck, clasping him to her with unexpected strength. If he stepped backwards, the move instinct now belatedly suggested, they would overbalance. He tried to pull away gently, without success. Her eyes were huge and dark in the moonlight, and quite unreadable.

"Oh Adam," she breathed, "you do love me after all."

"Miss Brennan . . ."

"You must call me Vanessa."

"Vanessa. I must apologize for insulting you so. I cannot think what came over me. Say you forgive me and let us—"

"Of course I forgive you, dearest Adam, for it was done in the heat of passion. Only say that you still respect me."

"I have the utmost respect for you, ma'am, but—"

"Then I accept your offer. What more can a girl ask in a husband than love, passion and respect?"

"I did not precisely offer for you!"

At last she released him and stepped away. "My lord, never say that you have been trifling with my affections? Oh, how shall I bear the shame!" Her voice held an edge of hysteria and tears gleamed on her cheeks.

"Miss Brennan—Vanessa!—it is all a misunderstanding . . ."

"Oh, Adam!" She cast herself into his arms again. "I knew you could not be so cruel. Let us go back to the house and announce our happiness to the world." She brushed his hair back from his brow.

"Lord, no. We cannot do that. Think how humiliating for Lady Catherine and Miss Davis, and Louise and Mary would be furious. Besides, I ought to address myself to your father."

"But Papa is gone to Vienna to prepare for the Congress."

"There you are, then! It would be most improper to announce our engagement before we have his permission. It must be a secret between us, and we must be careful not to let anyone guess."

"Not even Eliza?"

"Especially not Eliza. She'd never be able to resist triumphing over Louise and Mary. Promise me you will not tell?"

"Oh, very well, I will not tell. But if you are thinking of crying off . . ."

"Why should I think such a thing?" asked Adam blandly. "Come, my pet, or we shall miss the beginning of the next dance and that will be sure to arouse suspicion."

He delivered his betrothed to her next partner, then led Lady Catherine out onto the floor. He saw Sarah, sitting out a dance with his uncle, and carefully avoided meeting her eyes. Under his breath he cursed Vanessa Brennan.

Sarah watched Adam and Catherine performing with equal grace and expertise the complicated figures of the quadrille.

"Fine couple, an't they?" observed Sir Reginald. "The gal has dashed fine bloodlines, too. Earldom goes back to Henry VII, and it never hurts to add another earl to the family tree. What's more, she's no niminy-piminy miss he'd be bored with inside a month."

"You think Adam will choose Lady Catherine, sir?"

"Doubt it. The wench has a sharp tongue in her head and Adam's too softhearted for his own good. He don't like to hear her malice, though what's scandal without a spot of malice, I ask you?"

"Nothing, I am sure, sir. Is it true that Tsar Alexander insulted the Regent's favourite?"

Sir Reginald chuckled. "I was there when Prinny introduced Lady Hertford to him. He bowed without a word, then turned away muttering 'She is mighty old.' " He went on to regale her with gossip about the Regent's difficulties with his uncooperative royal guests.

Sarah listened with half her attention. Jonathan was dancing with Lydia for the second time, prompting her gently when she missed a step. As Sarah watched, he said something to the girl which made her laugh. Her usually solemn face lit and for a moment she was more beautiful than Vanessa would ever be. She really was the best of the three. Sarah was growing fond of her, and wished she would learn to be her natural self in Adam's presence.

The viscount and his partner crossed her view again. Though Adam was smiling, he looked tired and harassed. He had always risen nobly to the occasion in hosting his mother's balls, but Sarah knew he preferred a small party of friends to this display of the cream of the county. Lady Catherine was chattering brightly, apparently unaware of his distraction. She was not a sensitive person. Sarah was glad Sir Reginald thought his nephew would not choose the earl's daughter, for she could not like her.

Nor did she care for Vanessa's vanity, which absorbed her to the exclusion of all else. She had seen Adam escort Miss Brennan into the garden, but the girl's smug expression upon their return was not very different from her usual air of self-satisfaction. She was currently basking in Mr. Swanson's flow of compliments, unable to recognize their irony. Swan did not like Vanessa either.

"I think you are tired, m'dear," said Sir Reginald. "You ought to have laughed, or at least made some comment."

"I beg your pardon, sir. I was woolgathering, I fear. I am a little tired, for Saturday is generally a busy day with us. And tomorrow—today, rather—being Sunday, Jonathan and I plan to leave after this dance, or he will forget his sermon halfway through. Dare I ask you to repeat the story at which I ought to have laughed?"

"Impertinent puss." He chucked her under the chin. " 'Tis yet another tale of the Grand Duchess Catherine of Oldenburg, who has more impertinence in her little finger than you have in your whole charming body. She invited herself to a banquet at the Guildhall which was intended to be for gentlemen only. Prinny had hired the best Italian singers to entertain the company, and when they started up the Grand Duchess stopped them, saying that music made her nauseous. There wasn't a thing poor Prinny could do."

"She sounds a thoroughly unpleasant lady," said Sarah severely. "And now I must ask you to excuse me, sir, for the dance has ended and I see my brother coming to fetch me. Shall we see you in church tomorrow?"

His laugh rumbled out. "I may, perhaps, rise in time to attend evensong. Dashed if I don't, just for a glimpse of your pretty face. Good evening, Miss Meade."

As she and Jonathan went to take leave of Lady Cheverell, Sarah saw that Adam was already dancing again, with Jane. She hoped he was enjoying himself with the only sister who had no axe to grind.

After expressions of gratitude had been exchanged, for a delightful evening on one side, and for their attendance on the other, Lady Cheverell said apologetically, "I doubt there will be many at morning service tomorrow. I daresay the dancing will continue until dawn. I shall bring as many as I can to evensong."

"Your brother has promised to attend, ma'am."

"Reginald? Heavens above, he must be feeling his age. Integrations of mortality, you know."

"Well, perhaps promised is too strong a word. And from

what he said, his motives are not notably religious."

Lady Cheverell looked relieved. "I imagine he told you all he wanted was the sight of your pretty face," she said, with an unerring understanding of her brother. "Well, never mind that. We expect you to dinner on Monday, and Louise has organized an excursion to Salisbury on Tuesday. I cannot tell you what a help it has been to have you both practically members of the party. So difficult, always, with mostly family."

"I regret I shall be unable to go to Salisbury on Tuesday," Jonathan told her. "I have been neglecting my duties shamefully and must not spare a whole day."

"What a pity! But you will go, Sarah?"

Sarah exchanged a glance with her brother, who smiled indulgently and nodded.

"I ought to plead the same excuse," she said, "but I should love to go."

Knowing their plans, Gossett had already sent for the gig, so very soon they were driving back towards the village. At first Sarah was silent, wondering if she really did want to spend another whole day watching Adam at his wooing.

"Perhaps I should not go," she said tentatively. "It is true that I am falling behind on a hundred tasks. I have done nothing about my school."

"Enjoy yourself while you can," Jonathan advised. "The daily routine will return soon enough."

She took his words to heart, in a way he could scarcely have meant them. She would enjoy her friendship with Adam while he was still unattached, for no matter whom he married it must change their relationship for ever.

"I shall be glad to know you are along," her brother continued after a pause, "to keep an eye on Miss Davis. She is such a fragile child, and she trusts you even more than Louise."

"I cannot think that she will come to harm, but I shall certainly look out for her. I like her, do not you?"

"She is enchanting."

The depth of feeling in Jonathan's voice surprised Sarah. She hoped it meant no more than that his compassion had been aroused. Baron Davis of Clwyd, expecting a wealthy viscount for a son-in-law, was not at all likely to look favourably upon a poor country vicar.

Lord and Lady Lansdowne were two of those who went to church in Little Fittleton that Sunday. They had been invited to spend the night at Cheve after the ball, and were to stay till Monday morning so that the marquis and Adam could discuss politics.

Sarah was therefore prepared to find that the chief topic of conversation at dinner on Monday was politics. What she was not prepared for was Lady Catherine's part in the discussion. She seemed utterly oblivious of the fact that the Marquis of Lansdowne was a noted liberal, and that Adam's sympathies lay with the reformists. Her own views, though expressed with all the eloquence at her command, were mere repetition of her father's opinions, and the earl was a member of the most repressive Tory government in years.

Mary, aware of her brother's growing amusement, tried to silence her protégée by changing the subject.

"Of course the Corn Laws are necessary," she said, "or English farmers would cease to grow wheat and then we should not have any flour. This gâteau is quite delicious, Mama. I must have the receipt."

"Collecting receipts, Mary?" Adam enquired. His eyes

met Sarah's and she read mischief. "I did not know you frequented the kitchens."

"Naturally I do not, but I should not consider myself truly accomplished did I not know what goes forward there. A new receipt never comes amiss. Catherine knows that it will be her duty to supervise menus when she is married."

"And to keep household accounts," Lady Catherine added, eager to display yet one more talent. "Mama says they must be constantly checked or the servants and tradesmen will cheat without a second thought."

"I expect you know the price of flour, then."

"I know that it is a shocking price."

"Have you ever wondered why it is a shocking price, or how the poor pay that shocking price?"

"The poor are lazy good-for-nothings, or they would not be poor," pronounced Lady Catherine. "They can always go to the workhouses and be fed at public expense."

Adam caught Sarah's reproving glance, shrugged his shoulders and allowed Mary to change the subject. After dinner, when the gentlemen joined the ladies, he went straight to Sarah's side.

"That was cruel," she chided, "to lead the poor girl on to make a cake of herself."

"It would have been cruel had Lady Catherine experienced the least chagrin," he corrected. "She did not. She was simply expressing her opinions."

"But if she had guessed how you despise her opinions!"

"I knew she would not. She is incapable of understanding compassion, and therefore cannot understand that a reasonable man might differ from her views."

"Does she know about your charities?"

"She has never mentioned them, though I am sure Mary must have told her. She probably regards my work as one of those inexplicable whims gentlemen are prone to, which must be excused in an otherwise eligible husband."

Sarah laughed. Before she could speak, Louise interrupted their tête-à-tête.

"Adam, we are arranging transport for tomorrow. Do you mean to drive yourself?"

"Yes, I shall take my curricle and stop at the vicarage to pick up Sarah. We shall soon catch up with the rest of you, so there will be no need to block the village street with our cavalcade while you wait."

Five annoyed pairs of eyes turned on Sarah. She suppressed a sigh as she realized that Adam was once again using her as a buffer. When Mr. Swanson begged her to indulge him in a game of chess, she went with him gladly.

"I cannot think why you want to play with me," she said as they set up the pieces. "You beat me with greater ease every time we play. Surely my game ought to improve with practice?"

"Does," said Lord James, pulling up a chair to watch. "Just that Swan's gets better faster."

"So you are just using me for practice!" Sarah pretended indignation.

"Kerry, you wretch, you have given away my secret. Shall you refuse to play with me now, ma'am?"

"No, for if Lord James is telling the truth, at least my game is improving a little."

"Assure you, ma'am, wouldn't dream of lying to a lady!"

"And you need not fear that he was paying Spanish coin. Kerry wouldn't know a compliment if it bit him."

The game proceeded with much laughter and Sarah forgot her annoyance with Adam.

Chapter Fifteen

Adam had warned Sarah to expect him half an hour after the announced time the next morning, for with seven ladies to coordinate there was no hope of punctuality. She was ready when he pulled up in front of the vicarage, and she hurried out before he climbed down. He reached down to help her up.

"My strictures on the unpunctuality of females were not intended to include you," he observed as he gave his team the office.

"I am the exception that proves the rule? How flattering!"

"You are an exception to many rules, Sarah."

"If that is a compliment, it is a sadly dubious one." She wrinkled her nose at him. "I can think of any number of rules I should not care to break."

"Name one."

"Oh, the one that says that wisdom comes with age, for instance."

"It is I who must hope to conform to that rule. I have told you before that you are already wise despite your youth, have I not?"

"Yes, when I refrained from interfering between Jane and Lord Bradfield. That was common sense. Your horses are sweet-goers! Look, there are the other carriages already."

"I could wish that you had kept me waiting," said Adam as Swan and Kerry reined in their mounts and fell in on either side of the curricle.

They had company all the way to Amesbury, but a mile beyond the town, Adam halted at a crossroad.

"We are going via the lanes," he told his friends. "Miss Meade has a fancy to take the ribbons, and the main road is too busy."

"Splendid notion, we'll come, too," said Mr. Swanson.

"No, you will distract her attention from the horses," said the viscount firmly. "You go on with the others—and we shall meet you at the King's Arms." He swung the curricle down the right hand lane.

"I never expressed a wish to drive your team," protested Sarah. "I should not dare!"

"Tell me that you have no desire to try, and I shall turn around and apologize to Swan and Kerry for misleading them."

"Of course I should like to try, if you think they are not too strong for me. But this is scarcely the best place. This road winds along the Avon."

"The first part is straight enough. As for the horses, they have excellent manners and if you somehow succeed in making them bolt, I am here to stop them."

"Wretch! I do not expect to make them bolt."

"Take my gloves. Yours are too thin for driving." The leather gloves still held the warmth of his hands. Sarah made a determined effort to ignore the sense of intimacy which invaded her, and said with creditable lightness, "They are far too large. If I handle the reins clumsily, I shall blame it on them."

Concentrating on the horses, she forgot her momentary embarrassment. They were a pleasure to drive, responding to the slightest touch, unlike Dapple who went his own pace no matter what he was told. She drove through the village of Great Durnford, then handed the reins, and the gloves, back to Adam when they reached the bends along the river.

It was a beautiful July day. The water meadows were lush and green, the hedgerows full of honeysuckle and travellers' joy. Sarah sat back, content to enjoy the peaceful scene, and a companionable silence fell between them.

The soaring spire of Salisbury Cathedral was already visible when they passed a crossroad with a lane leading up the hill to their left.

"Have you ever been to Old Sarum?" Sarah asked. "I have passed the turn a hundred times and never gone up."

"Jonathan and I went when we were boys, out riding. There is little to be seen but the ruins of the castle, and not much of that, though there is a marvellous view of the cathedral. Should you like to go now?"

"Another day. We must not keep everyone waiting. I am glad you let me take the reins, or I should not know how to face Kerry and Swan."

"Kerry and Swan? I had not realized you were on such terms with them." Adam's voice was austere.

"I do not address them so, but surely when I speak to you there can be no harm in calling them as you do."

"It is a deal too familiar," he snapped. "Oh, I'm sorry, Sarah. I do not mean to criticize. I am only concerned lest you be hurt, for those two are without a doubt the most confirmed bachelors on the town."

"I cannot see that that has anything to do with what I call them. You surely do not suppose that I expect an offer from either, let alone both." Sarah tried to turn his unexpected remonstrance into a joke. "Now your concern might

143

be justified if I were to address his lordship as James, or Mr. Swanson as Frederick."

"You are right, I am building a mountain out of a molehill. Forgive me, and pray do not start to call him Freddy!"

When they reached Salisbury and rejoined the others, it was decided to tour the cathedral first. Preoccupied by the mystery of Adam's strange behaviour, Sarah followed the group around the cathedral without the least interest in what she was looking at. She knew the place well, knew in advance every spot where Lady Catherine would insist on stopping to sketch some point of particular importance. At last the artist was overruled by a majority who considered enough time had been spent there.

"There are many other interesting buildings in the town, from every period of history," said Louise firmly. "You can draw them while the rest of us look at the shops."

"I must take an impression of the entire cathedral from outside," Lady Catherine protested.

Even Mary objected to this. "It is far too large for a close view," she pointed out.

"Adam said there is an excellent view from Old Sarum," said Sarah without thinking.

Adam threw her a reproachful glance as Lady Catherine seized the excuse to hang on his arm and question him.

The gentlemen opted to retire for a tankard of ale at the King's Arms, the Tudor inn where Charles II's escape to France had been plotted.

"Thirsty work, looking at churches," Lord James confided to Sarah.

She nodded in agreement, for she would have been glad of a cup of tea, but the rest of the ladies were eager to investigate Salisbury's drapers and milliners and mantua-makers.

With Adam gone, Lady Catherine lost interest in sketching, passing the fourteenth century Old George Inn without a second glance. Sarah had no money in her purse and she soon grew bored. It was then she realized Lydia was missing.

"I expect she misunderstood our plans and went back to the King's Arms with the gentlemen," said Louise, when this was drawn to her attention. "Depend upon it, she is safe there with Adam." She looked complacent.

"I cannot be easy," Sarah said. "I shall go and make sure she is there."

The gentlemen were in the taproom, where Lydia would have been neither welcome nor comfortable. The innkeeper sent Adam out to Sarah, and they decided to go back to the cathedral, that being the last place anyone remembered seeing Miss Davis. Recalling her promise to Jonathan, Sarah felt guilty as well as worried and she rushed Adam through the busy streets and the quiet close.

Inside the cathedral the lofty nave echoed with the sound of choir and organ. Lydia was sitting near the back, a slight figure absorbed in the beauty of the music. Sarah had to touch her shoulder before she noticed them. It seemed sacrilegious to tear her away, but she followed them out quite willingly.

"I knew you would find me," she said. "I was not afraid. Mr. Meade told me he was ordained here, and then the choir started practising. I am sorry if I have caused any trouble."

Adam smiled at this disjointed speech and said gently, "I can quite understand how the music captivated you. I hope you will not be angry with us for interrupting."

"Oh no, my lord, how could I be? Lady Edward will call me a ninnyhammer for wandering off alone."

"I shall not let Louise abuse you," said the viscount gallantly. "We had best head back now, however, before she begins to worry." He offered an arm to each lady. "Tell us about the music."

As they walked back to the King's Arms, Lydia talked knowledgeably of Bach and Palestrina and Handel. The governess who had taught her to sing had often taken her to hear the choir and organ at Hereford Cathedral, near her home. Neither Sarah nor Adam had any great interest in church music but they listened indulgently. Sarah was delighted that at last Lydia was losing her nervousness.

Her animation died as soon as they joined the others, who were by now all gathered at the inn for luncheon. Flushed to the roots of her hair she apologized in a thread of a voice for boring his lordship with her prattle and fled to Louise's side. Sarah felt like shaking her.

After luncheon, they strolled by the river while Lady Catherine sketched the medieval bridges. She kept Adam at her side with a flood of questions about the town. He had learned quite a lot as a boy, from Sarah and Jonathan's father, but when he did not know the answers he made them up, growing more and more outrageous. Lady Catherine accepted his version of history without a blink, until he told her that James Wyatt had thrown cartloads of ancient stained glass into the city ditch during his renovation of the cathedral.

"You are hoaxing me, my lord," she accused with a roguish smile. "James Wyatt was a famous architect. I cannot believe that he was such a Philistine."

The story happened to be true, but Adam saw no need to enlighten her. He wanted to tell Sarah how he had played on Lady Catherine's gullibility, to hear Sarah laugh and scold him. He looked longingly after the rest of the party

146

and heard not a word of Catherine's next speech.

"By all means," he said agreeably when he became aware that she was waiting for an answer. It seemed a safe enough comment, but over the next few minutes he realized that he had somehow promised to drive her home in his curricle by way of Old Sarum.

At first he was furious, but then he reconsidered. He had enjoyed the drive to Salisbury, yet the ominous knowledge of his betrothal to Vanessa Brennan had been with him all the way. It might be better to avoid being alone with Sarah until he had resolved that business, though how it was to be resolved he had no notion.

The rest of the party was walking back towards them. Adam suddenly wondered what Sarah would think when he announced that he was to take up someone else for the return journey. Her feelings, so often dismissed with a cavalier "Sarah won't mind," were now of the utmost importance to him. He decided to explain to her privately how it had come about.

"I shall tell your sister Mary our plan," said Lady Catherine, packing up her sketching materials.

That proposal suited him very well. Mary could inform the others when it became necessary, and in the meantime he would have a chance to mend his fences with Sarah. Then, when everyone met at Old Sarum, he would abandon Lady Catherine to her pencils and easel while he showed Sarah the castle ruins.

They all walked back through the busy streets to the King's Arms to drink tea before their departure. On the way, Adam saw Lady Catherine draw Mary a little aside from the rest and speak to her earnestly. He accomplished the same manoeuvre with Sarah, though their conversation was anything but earnest. As he expected, she laughed at him and then took him to task for misleading Catherine with his wild tales.

"But she is revenged," he went on. "During a moment's inattention, I was gulled into agreeing to drive her back to Cheve. You can imagine my mortification when I realized what she had asked me."

He thought Sarah's smile was a little strained, but she answered calmly enough, "No doubt Mary will be *aux anges.*"

After tea, Adam's curricle drove first out of Salisbury. Lady Catherine encouraged the viscount to show his team's paces, and when they reached the turn to Old Sarum the other carriages were out of sight behind them. He would have waited at the crossroads, but she pointed out that the sooner they reached the ruins, the shorter time she would keep everyone waiting while she sketched. Surprised at her consideration, he turned off the main road, and a few minutes later they alighted at the top of the hill overlooking the city.

It was a bare and windswept place. That was one of the reasons, as Adam had truthfully told Catherine, the bishop's see had been moved to the valley in the thirteenth century. He tethered the horses to a bush, then they found seats on the fallen stones of the Norman castle. The view of the cathedral and chequerboard town was spectacular.

Lady Catherine set up her easel, while Adam waited impatiently for the others to arrive. Twenty minutes passed, and there was no sign of the carriages. Adam paced restlessly, pausing at frequent intervals to gaze down the lane and check his pocket watch. His companion seemed wholly absorbed in her artistic endeavours.

"Where the devil are they?" he burst out at last.

"Oh, my lord!"

"I beg your pardon, but don't turn missish on me now! We have been here nearly an hour and it is scarce half a mile from the main road. They cannot have lost their way."

"Perhaps they missed the turning," suggested Lady Catherine with an agitated air, rising to her feet. "Or perhaps . . . Surely not! Perhaps Mary misunderstood our intentions and they have gone back to Cheve House without us. Would that you had brought a groom, my lord! We have been alone together in this deserted place for so long, I fear that my reputation will be shockingly compromised."

"Fustian," said the viscount bracingly. "It is perfectly proper for a young lady to drive about the countryside with a gentleman in an open carriage."

"To be sure, if we had not strayed from the high-road. I dread to think what Papa will say when he hears of this. Papa holds himself very high, you know, and cannot abide the least suggestion of impropriety. Alas, he is all too likely to cast doubt upon your honour, my lord!"

The glimmering of an idea seized Adam. As well be hanged for a sheep as a lamb. Sarah, in one of her adorable flights of fancy, had accused him of wanting to set up his harem. Well, this was England, not Turkey, and nobody could force him to marry two females at once.

"The earl cannot doubt my honour if we tell him we are to be wed," he said with reckless abandon.

"On the contrary, he will be delighted." Lady Catherine was calm. "It is in every way an eligible connection. To be sure, my rank is higher, but your family is nearly as ancient and I am given to understand . . . That, is of course, the settlements are between you and Papa. I shall write and tell him the good news at once. You may kiss me, Cheverell." She took a step toward him.

"I cannot think that wise, considering our present situation." He backed away. "That is, I must not take advantage of you by accepting your kind offer, but it will be equally unwise to publish our news too soon. You will not want it to be said that I offered only because you were compromised. Besides, I cannot like to disappoint Miss Brennan and Miss Davis, and Louise and Eliza would make my life deuced uncomfortable. In fact, it is particularly important that you do not tell Mary, for she is bound to let it slip to her sisters. Let us wait until after the end of the house party."

She considered. "Perhaps it will be best. I confess, I should prefer not to tell Papa that we were stranded together in the depths of the countryside. Of course, if it should later prove necessary, I shall not hesitate to disclose everything."

"Why should it ever be necessary?" asked Adam blandly.

When at last they drove through Little Fittleton, past the vicarage, Adam knew that everyone else must have reached home long since. He could only hope that Sarah was at the back of the vicarage, unable to see his late arrival with the triumphant Lady Catherine at his side.

Chapter Sixteen

✦✦ ✦✦

Sarah had not seen the curricle drive past, but she learned of its delayed return the next morning. Lady Cheverell, on her way to visit a neighbour, called at the vicarage.

"My dear, I bear another invitation," she announced. "Such a gay time as we are having! Louise has planned a picnic for tomorrow, if the weather holds fine, at the cumuli over by Tilshead."

A glorious, if momentary, vision of ladies and gentlemen picnicking among the clouds crossed Sarah's mind before she realized her visitor was referring to the prehistoric tumuli scattered across Salisbury Plain.

"A banquet among the burial mounds? An interesting notion."

"Adam has praised Lydia Davis's riding, you see, so Louise wanted to choose somewhere that can only be reached on horseback."

"But you and Sir Reginald will not be able to go."

"We old folks will be quite content to stay home and gossip, my dear. I passed the age for picnics long since, and it is Louise's turn to parade her protégée. Miss Brennan showed to advantage at the ball, and Lady Catherine had her chance in Salisbury. I quite thought she had made the most of it, too, when they returned so late yesterday, until I learned they had stopped here to ensure that you had

151

reached home safely. Well, I must be on my way. Shall you go tomorrow?"

"I would not miss it for the world," said Sarah grimly.

It was the outside of enough that Adam had used her as an excuse for dallying with Lady Catherine, especially after pretending he was reluctant to drive the girl home. Sarah had every intention of taking him to task for it. However, he did not call that day. Swan and Kerry, who dropped in for half an hour, said that he was gone out on estate business. They accepted a glass of Madeira and ate all Mrs. Hicks's fresh-baked shortbread.

"I say," remarked Kerry wistfully, eyeing the empty plate, "that was deuced good. Don't suppose your cook would let us make gingerbread men again one day? Haven't had so much fun since I don't know when."

"You haven't made so long a speech in the presence of a lady since I don't know when," Mr. Swanson said in surprise.

"Miss Meade ain't like other females." His eyes turned to Sarah with a hopeful devotion that reminded her of a puppy begging for a walk.

"I'll ask Mrs. Hicks," she promised, smiling. "I cannot suppose she will have any objection."

When the gentlemen took their leave, Swan drew her aside for a moment.

"You're doing poor Kerry a world of good," he told her, his voice serious. "He managed to answer Lady Bradfield without blushing the other day. He's right, you're not like other females. Dashed sight kinder than most, for one thing. I'm glad I came down with Adam or I'd never have had a chance to make your acquaintance."

There was a thoughtful expression on Sarah's face as she watched them ride down the village street.

★ ★ ★ ★ ★

The next day dawned sunny but with a brisk breeze chivvying a few cumulus clouds across the sky like frightened sheep. It was perfect weather for riding across the hills. Nonetheless, Adam had distinct misgivings about the proposed outing. Yesterday he had managed to avoid seeing either of the young ladies to whom he was engaged, except in company. However, a party on horseback was bound to straggle and both would undoubtedly expect him to stay close to them.

Quite apart from other considerations, the thought of plodding along beside Miss Brennan or risking his neck with Lady Catherine was enough to ruin his day.

Lady Catherine unwittingly solved his problem when she sought him out in the library, where he had retired to ponder his fate after breakfast. She glanced around, saw that he was alone, and dropped the three books she was carrying on a table.

"There," she said with satisfaction. "Everyone will suppose that I am merely looking for something to read. I declare I am quite enjoying our little deception, Cheverell. It is just like acting in a play." She leaned over his chair and brushed back the lock of hair from his forehead.

"And a very fine actress you are, ma'am," Adam hastened to assure her, "but you had best keep your distance lest someone comes in. I am sure no one has the least notion of our secret, and it would be the greatest pity to waste your efforts. Much as it disappoints me, I must not make you the object of any particular attentions today."

Her vanity thus appealed to, she agreed. She took a couple of books from the shelves and departed holding them before her in an exaggerated attempt to disguise her purpose. Adam breathed a sigh of relief and went to look for Miss Brennan.

Unlike Catherine, Vanessa had never prided herself upon her acting ability, so she was somewhat surprised to be congratulated upon it. Adam had to add a suggestion that close proximity might make it impossible for him to keep his hands off her, which had the merit of being per-fectly true. He wanted to put them around her neck. At last, still pouting, she agreed to accept his apparent neglect. He went off to make last-minute arrangements for mounts for his guests, with plans for separating Sarah from them floating in his head.

His plans were doomed to failure. From the moment they reached the vicarage and Sarah mounted the docile mare he had chosen for her, Swan and Kerry stuck like leeches on either side of her. He did not dare single her out by attempting to displace her cavaliers. As he rode behind the merry trio, his irritation grew as he noted how at ease his friends, even Kerry, seemed to be with her.

Distracted as he was, his eldest sister found it easy to en-sure that Miss Davis was at his side when they left the vil-lage behind.

The horses spread out, finding their way across the trackless turf in small groups. Sarah's two besotted swains, both bruising riders, kept pace with her cautious canter. She sat straight and slim in her grey habit, but to Adam's searching gaze there was a certain tension in her bearing. He vowed to make it his business to see that she rode regu-larly in future, as long as she lived in Little Fittleton.

Jonathan, with Christian forbearance, lagged behind at a walk beside Miss Brennan, while Lady Catherine galloped ahead with Mary and her husband. All in all, Adam was not displeased to ride with Miss Davis, suiting their pace to the terrain. She was not an enlivening companion, but at present he felt more in need of soothing, and it was a relief not to have to make conversation. She was more than satisfied with his occasional remark about the fineness of the day or the beauty of wide horizons uncluttered with trees.

The barrows rose from the plain ahead, low, green hills too steep-sided and regular in shape to be natural. Adam remembered iron-age battles he and Jonathan had fought here, with Sarah unwillingly cast as the captive princess or, if she protested strongly at that rôle, as the invading Roman army, doomed to defeat.

He wanted to wander with her among the burial mounds, reminiscing. Instead, he helped Miss Davis down from her horse and escorted her to where the grooms sent ahead from Cheve had spread rugs and cushions in the shade of a solitary yew.

Mary and Lady Catherine were already unpacking the hampers the grooms had brought, producing veal-and-ham pie, cold chicken, cheeses, cherries, bread and wine and lemonade. Miss Davis went to help, and Adam stood chatting with Mary's husband, watching as the rest of the party rode up. He would have gone to help Sarah dismount but she avoided looking at him and accepted Kerry's aid with every evidence of pleasure. Adam was shocked by the lance of fury that stabbed through him at the sight of her hands on Kerry's shoulders, his at her waist, her smile as he swung her down.

He turned back to invite Miss Davis to sit beside him, and plied her with food until she was quite bewildered. He tried not to look at Sarah, but it was impossible not to be conscious of her presence. She seemed to him to be flirting wildly, in a most uncharacteristic and unbecoming manner, with Swan and Kerry. Trying to persuade himself that what he was feeling was not jealousy but concern for her disappointment when neither came up to scratch, he absently offered Miss Davis a third red-currant tart.

Her timid refusal drew his attention at last. He looked down to see her plate piled high with untouched delicacies.

"Not hungry?" he asked with a kind smile. "Nor am I. Shall we go for a stroll?" All he wanted was to remove himself from Sarah's vicinity.

"If . . . if Lady Edward says I may." There was a hint of alarm in Miss Davis's expression.

Adam had not the slightest doubt of his sister's approval, and he was proved right. The alarm on Miss Davis's face deepened as Louise whispered to her, and she returned to Adam with a faltering step. As they moved away from the picnickers, he set about relieving her apprehension.

"Jonathan and I used to come here often on our ponies when we were children," he told her. He described their battles in a way calculated to make her laugh, and at last succeeded in winning a smile.

With a little coaxing she was soon chattering happily about the misdeeds of her brothers. She had an instinctive understanding of and sympathy for childish mischief that Adam found most attractive. He could imagine her, grown older and more poised, as a superb mother. It was a great pity that he had not the slightest desire to make her the mother of his own children.

They were out of sight of the others by now, and approaching a barrow somewhat smaller and less steep than most.

"I think this is the place where I was buried," he said. "I was a heroic Briton, a war chieftain grievously wounded fighting the Romans. Jonathan was my high priest and we invented an elaborate funeral ceremony involving a sacrificial maiden. Poor Sarah played that part, of course, though she did not like it one bit. We tried to dig a grave on top of this mound, without great success. I wonder if there is any sign left of our digging."

"Let us go and see," suggested Miss Davis with unexpected enthusiasm. "Then I shall be able to describe it properly to the boys when I go home."

The girl refused any assistance, shying away when Adam offered his hand. When they reached the top after a breathless scramble which brought a delightful colour to her cheeks, the green grass showed no sign of any disturbance. They stood for a moment admiring the view, then started back down the steep slope.

Again she refused help. Adam went ahead, glancing back anxiously as she picked her way down from tussock to tussock, the train of her habit draped over one arm. Sarah had been in short skirts when they had come here as children, and he had not realized how awkward the climb could be for a female.

He waited at the bottom, and she was no more than a dozen feet above him when she lost her balance. Arms waving in an attempt to recover herself, she dropped her train, caught her foot in it, and slithered the rest of the way to land in a heap at his feet.

He reached down to help her up. Her face was white.

"I've turned my ankle," she whispered. "It will be all right in a minute, I expect." She moved to sit up, wincing and biting her lip.

"We'd best take your boot off at once, in case it swells," said Adam, suiting action to the words despite her protest. "Lord, you won't be able to walk on this."

"It will be better directly. I . . . I'm sorry, my lord."

"Nonsense! It is entirely my fault, and I shall do penance

by carrying you back. How fortunate that you are a mere slip of a girl." He grinned at her encouragingly as he lifted her in his arms and started back towards the others.

"Oh no, please, put me down. I can walk, indeed I can." The colour of her face fluctuated from white to scarlet and back again. Fright and embarrassment mingled in her eyes and her slight body trembled with tension. "It cannot be proper for you to carry me, my lord. Pray let me try to walk."

"That will only do you a further injury. Try to relax, Lydia. Lay your head on my shoulder."

"I cannot! Oh, what will everyone think? I cannot bear to face them."

"They will think me a fool for letting you climb the barrow," he said, with what patience he could muster.

Tears began to trickle down her pale cheeks. "They will think me the veriest hoyden, and quite lost to all shame."

"No one can hold you to blame for your accident, but if anyone takes exception to your being in my arms, you had best tell them we are betrothed."

The tears ceased and she looked up at him in amazement. "Betrothed? But you cannot wish to marry me."

"Do stop telling me what I can and cannot do, there's a pet."

"Do you really mean it?" she asked doubtfully. "Lady Edward will be happy, and Papa and Mama."

"And you?"

"I . . . I expect I shall grow used to the idea. Mama says I will like to be a viscountess and have lots of pin money."

"I am sure you will. Now, lay your head on my shoulder and relax. It is very difficult to carry you when I feel you may jump down at any moment."

She obeyed. "Are we truly betrothed, then? It seems very strange."

It seemed strange to Adam, too, though he was beginning to grow accustomed to the feeling. After all, it was his third betrothal within a week. There was safety in numbers, he reminded himself, doing his best to suppress an inner voice that told him this time was different.

"This is excessively romantic," sighed Lydia. "If only my ankle did not ache so. Do you really think people will not be shocked that you are carrying me?"

"They will be by far too concerned about your injury. I daresay there will be a great to-do and we will not even have a chance to tell them about being engaged to be married."

"Oh yes, let us keep it a secret. That will be even more romantic, will it not? Just like something out of a novel."

Adam breathed a silent sigh of relief.

Chapter Seventeen

Sarah lost interest in flirting with Lord James and Mr. Swanson as soon as Adam was out of sight.

Though she tried to conceal it, the spirit went out of her repartee.

"Care to take a stroll?" suggested Swan with a knowing look in his eye. "There's nothing like a little gentle exercise after overeating."

"Speak for yourself!" said Kerry indignantly. "Miss Meade ain't overeaten. Eats like a sparrow."

"Thank you, my lord," Sarah laughed. "Nonetheless, I should like to walk for a while. I have not been here for years."

Kerry jumped up and gave her a hand. "Deuced peculiar notion, if you ask me, having a party in a graveyard."

"Hush, there's a good fellow." Mr. Swanson struggled to his feet. "You wouldn't want Lady Edward to hear you."

His friend glanced round in alarm. Sarah patted his arm soothingly.

"Louise is far too busy preening herself on throwing Adam and Lydia together to care what you say." Her voice was dry. "We must not spoil her triumph. Let us go this way."

She led them in the opposite direction, regaling them with the same tales of battle that Adam was telling Lydia.

Swan was thoroughly amused, but Kerry grew quite indignant when her rôle as sacrificial victim was explained to him.

"Never would have thought it of Adam," he said in puzzlement, "nor your brother neither, ma'am. Obliging fellows in the general way, I assure you."

"Did you have no sisters to tease when you were a boy, sir?"

"They teased me," he explained gloomily. "Never got the chance to turn the tables. Still afraid of m'sisters."

"Formidable females," Swan agreed.

They wandered back to the picnic site. Lord Edward and Mary's husband were dozing among the cushions, while Louise and Jonathan chatted nearby. Everyone else had gone to stroll among the barrows. Sarah started making daisy chains, and her companions persuaded her to teach them the art. Soon she was festooned with necklaces and bracelets and crowned with several wreaths of the pink-tipped flowers. She was laughingly protesting the addition of yet another, when Adam appeared with Lydia in his arms.

She jumped up, scattering flowers across the rugs, and hurried towards them.

"What happened? Lydia, are you hurt?"

"Miss Davis slipped and turned her ankle. I fear it is badly swollen."

"My dear, is it very painful? You are a little pale. Set her down on the cushions, Adam, and I will look at it."

The others crowded round with expressions of sympathy until Louise chased the gentlemen off. Lydia had not said a word but she could not suppress a cry of pain when Sarah touched her ankle with gentle fingers in an attempt to discover the extent of the injury.

161

"You cannot possibly ride home," said Sarah, frowning in thought.

"Adam shall take her before him on Caesar," Louise proposed with a pleased smile.

"Oh no, I could not. Pray do not make me," Lydia beseeched her, flushing.

Eliza and Lord Moffatt and Vanessa Brennan hurried up at that moment. Eliza was firmly of the opinion that it would be most improper for Lydia to ride with Adam. The sisters were beginning to squabble when Sarah cut across their argument.

"I believe my brother is the best person to take her. As he is a clergyman there cannot be the least suggestion of impropriety. Jonathan!" she called. "You will not mind carrying Miss Davis before you?"

He left the group of gentlemen who were standing about looking uncomfortable at their uselessness.

"I shall be glad to be of assistance." He looked down at the girl with a warm smile. "The sooner we have you safely home the better," he suggested. "Will you come with me?"

"Oh yes, I shall not mind going with you, sir. Sarah, will you come with me?"

Louise said sulkily that she would go too, and Lord Edward elected to accompany them, while Adam stayed behind to round up the rest of the party and escort them back to Cheve. Sarah glanced back as they rode off. Swan and Kerry were looking after her wistfully, and she realized that in the bustle of taking care of Lydia she had abandoned them without a thought.

Adam was also watching their departure. His expression was enigmatic. Sarah was suddenly afraid that he resented her interference, that he had wanted to hold Lydia in his arms on Caesar's back as he had carried her from the scene of her accident. A wave of pure jealousy flooded through her. Was it possible that Adam had a tendre for the girl?

She did not see him again that day, and when she woke the next morning her emotions were still in turmoil. She was also somewhat stiff from riding. The best cure for both conditions, she decided, was a walk to Stonehenge.

There was a damp chill in the air when she slipped out of bed. She shivered as she drew back the curtains and looked out into grey nothingness. A damp, gloomy shroud of mist hid the church; she could scarcely make out the low stone wall separating the garden from the churchyard. It was no day for walking freely across the hills, yet she could not bear the thought of being confined to the house. She put on an old brown walking dress and took a warm cloak downstairs with her.

Jonathan had been unusually silent the previous evening and he was no more communicative that morning. Having assured himself that his sister meant to stick to the lanes, he returned to his newspaper. She ate a piece of toast and drank some tea, then put an apple in her pocket and set out.

The only sign of life in the street was a scavenging mongrel. The village seemed unfamiliar and vaguely ominous in its grey stillness and Sarah was glad to leave it behind her. Though she could see only a few paces to either side, the lane that led towards Amesbury and Stonehenge was clearly defined in white chalk against the green grass and she had no fear of losing her way. The mist muffled the sound of her footsteps and neither birdsong nor bleating sheep broke the silence.

Warmed by the exercise, she was throwing back the hood of her cloak when she heard the drumming of hooves close behind her.

"Sarah!"

She looked up into Adam's smiling eyes as he drew rein beside her. Her heart turned over.

With effortless grace he swung down from Caesar's saddle to walk beside her, leading the horse.

"Lord, it's difficult to find you alone!" he said.

"Did you want to?" She felt ridiculously shy.

"Desperately." He reached for her hand, then drew back, his smile fading. "What a devilish coil," he groaned. "I am at my wits' end."

"What is it?" Sarah's sympathy had a cautious note. "Never tell me that Marguerite has returned to haunt you, or did you meet Peggy in the village? I had thought her resigned to losing her hero."

"Much worse. I scarcely know how to tell you."

"Then pray do not."

"I must. You are my only hope and I could not bear it if you found out from someone else. Sarah, I'm engaged."

Shock froze her, her gaze on his despairing face. Then she looked away, drew a deep breath and walked on.

"To whom?" Her voice was carefully neutral.

"To Lydia . . ."

"I wondered, yesterday. She is a very sweet girl. I wish you happy, Adam."

". . . and to Vanessa . . ."

"Vanessa!"

". . . and Catherine."

Sarah laughed. She could not help herself. She heard her own hysteria and could not stop.

Adam took her by the shoulders and shook her. "Don't," he pleaded. "Please don't." As her laughter died, he bent his head and kissed her very gently on the lips, a fleeting touch. "I'm sorry, Sarah. Tell me what to do."

"Tell me how it happened."

164

They walked on, her hand on his arm warm between his elbow and his side. She listened with a sense of unreality, increased by their isolation in the mist, as he explained how Vanessa had lured him into the garden and Catherine had trapped him at Old Sarum.

"I never actually proposed to either of them," he pointed out. "I merely let them believe I conceded."

"Such a scandalous want of conduct, and I thought them such proper young ladies," she marvelled. "I cannot believe that Lydia is either brave enough or unprincipled enough to have set a like snare."

"No, I cannot claim that excuse. Her fall was undoubtedly accidental and her injury genuine. She was quite overset by the intimacy of her position in my arms, afraid of what everyone would say. I suggested that if we were betrothed it would cause no comment and the notion soothed her sensibilities. I could not retract after that. Besides, I confess that three prospective brides seemed to me little worse than two, though I've not the least desire to wed any of them."

"How did you persuade her not to tell?"

"She thought a secret betrothal the most romantic thing in the world, just like a novel," said Adam dryly. "What surprises me is that none of my sisters has attempted to discover what went on on those three occasions."

"I have no doubt that none of them wished to draw attention to their connivance in entrapping you. Eliza's part in forcing you into the garden is obvious to the meanest intelligence. Mary must surely be responsible for not informing the rest of us about your detour to Old Sarum, though she may have believed your bouncer about stopping at the vicarage on your way home."

"*My* bouncer? Is your opinion of me so low? That was

purely Lady Catherine's invention. I wanted to wring her wretched neck but the dictates of gentlemanly behaviour prevented my even giving her the lie."

Sarah felt as if a great weight had lifted from her spirits. The situation was unchanged, yet her view of it had altered radically. Resentment and indignation faded and she found herself amused at his predicament.

"Of course, I should have guessed. I daresay she considered it part of her playacting. How fortunate for you that writing and performing plays is another of her innumerable talents! Are you sure you do not wish to wed so admirably accomplished a young lady?"

"I have never been more certain of anything in my life," Adam declared roundly, delighted to hear the teasing note in her voice. "Nor do I wish to spend my days gazing on Vanessa's exquisite beauty. But how the devil am I to extricate myself?"

She laughed, the merry laugh with a hint of mischief in it that he loved to hear. The mists were thinning now, swirling about them, and a sunbeam broke through. Droplets of water in her hair gleamed as golden as the flecks in her eyes, and he knew that hers was a face he would never tire of.

Her next words brought him abruptly back to earth.

"I shall help you cast off Catherine and Vanessa without a qualm after their disgraceful behaviour," she said seriously. "Lydia is another matter. She is an innocent child and I will not be party to disappointing her. I think you are going to have to marry her, Adam."

He looked at her in helpless dismay: All at once the various strands of their relationship came together in his mind: the old, comfortable friendship; the new admiration of her subtle beauty; his jealousy of Swan and Kerry; the feeling that something was missing when he was not with her; and the urge to take her in his arms when she was near and smother her with kisses. This explained his willingness to dismiss all his mistresses and his inability to choose another. There was only one woman in the world he wanted and he wanted her to be his forever.

He had lost his heart to Sarah, and here she was, explaining to him why he must marry Miss Lydia Davis. What was infinitely worse was that he knew she was right: he could not honourably cry off.

Chapter Eighteen

Adam's abrupt departure puzzled Sarah. After making her promise that she would not stray from the road, lest the mist close down again, he had ridden off without a backward glance. She walked on slowly, deep in thought.

There was no understanding men. She had insisted on his obligation to Lydia partly in the hope of discovering how he felt about taking the bashful child to wife. She still had no notion whether he was despondent, resigned, or even content to have the decision made for him. Her other aim, she acknowledged to herself, was to punish him a little for his blithe disregard of convention. The trouble was that all her arguments were true. He had no excuse whatsoever for retracting his proposal.

Though she had always told herself that she had no hope of winning him, Sarah's heart sank at the finality of his engagement. It was no use trying to persuade herself that no woman of sense could possibly love a man who flitted from female to female like a bee from blossom to blossom. Common sense had nothing to do with it.

An idea nagged at her. One man, many brides . . . Bluebeard! Catherine and Vanessa must surely know the fairy tale, so that she would not have to be too explicit. If she could give them a disgust of Adam, they might release him of their own accord. It would not hurt to make them ashamed of their own deceit while she was about it, and she had an idea how to go about that, too.

Her eyes sparkling with mischief, Sarah swung round and started back towards Little Fittleton. The sooner she put her plan into action the better, for there was no knowing when one of the young ladies might let the cat out of the bag and precipitate a horrendous scandal.

It was still early. Even after stopping at the vicarage to change her dress, Sarah arrived at Cheve House before all the ladies had left their chambers. She asked for Lady Cheverell, and Gossett showed her into the morning room.

"Sarah, my dear, how delightful to see you. Oh dear, I am growing so forgetful. Have we an outing planned for today?"

"No, ma'am, and it is shockingly early for a morning call. I had a sudden whim to go shopping in Devizes and I wondered whether Lady Catherine and Miss Brennan might care to go, too. Miss Davis's ankle will prevent her joining us, I collect?"

"The poor child is much improved but she had best rest it today." She rang the bell. "I must confess, I shall be very glad if you will take the other two off for the day. I cannot like them, Sarah! If Adam weds one of them, I shall happily retire to the dower house in Salisbury."

The butler was sent to enquire whether the young ladies were interested in a shopping excursion. This was the weakest part of Sarah's scheme. Mary and Eliza had warned their protégées not to offend the Meades, but if they felt themselves secure in having caught Adam, they might ignore the advice. However, Gossett returned shortly with two acceptances.

"Then it remains only to beg the use of your barouche," said Sarah gaily, trying to conceal her relief. "It is sadly forward in me, I know, but I fear Lady Catherine and Miss Brennan will change their minds if I offer to drive them in the gig behind Dapple."

"To be sure, their gowns would be horridly crushed and that will never do. You will not want to drive the barouche, though. One of the grooms shall take you."

This was a difficulty Sarah had not foreseen. It was quite unsuitable for her to sit on the box, besides making it impossible to converse with her passengers, yet she did not want a groom listening while she denounced his master. Then she remembered Nellie's follower, who was so eager to please his sweetheart's employers.

"If Peter is available," she requested, "I should prefer him. I know him for a trustworthy lad." And discreet, she hoped.

Not an hour later, Peter was driving the barouche north toward Devizes with three young ladies seated behind him. Sarah explained to her guests that the opening of the Kennet-Avon Canal some four years since had greatly increased the prosperity of the town, leading to the establishment of many new shops.

"Lady Lansdowne told me of a milliner she considers the equal of any in London." As she hoped, this led to a lengthy discussion of fashion from which she was largely excluded. She planned to introduce the subject of Adam on the way home, for she had no intention of escorting two sulky young ladies all day.

Sarah found touring the shops of Devizes with Lady Catherine and Vanessa Brennan unspeakably tedious. Nothing came up to London standards except Lady Lansdowne's milliner (being a marchioness she was not to be contradicted), where each bought a bonnet. Sarah's feet were aching by the time they returned to the Bear for refreshments before leaving for Cheve.

They sat at the window overlooking the bustling market-place. Sarah enquired of the waitress whether the tall stone monument in the centre of the square was the market cross recently erected by Lord Sidmouth to commemorate his long association with the town.

"Yes'm, thet be it. Ha' ye heard the story?" The girl set down a tray of tea and buns.

"I have, but I should like to read it for myself."

"What story is that?" clamoured her companions. Sarah refused to tell, claiming that she feared to relate it incorrectly. It was time to put into effect the first part of her plan, to make them ashamed of their dishonest stratagems. She turned the conversation to the ball at Cheve and the outing to Salisbury, thus ensuring that the discreditable events of each occasion were at the forefront of their minds. Tea finished and a message sent to Peter that they would require the carriage in twenty minutes, they strolled over to the market cross.

Built of stone, it was some twenty feet high with four turrets on top, an impressive monument. In a niche on one side they found inscribed the tale Sarah was looking for.

" 'The Mayor and Corporation of Devizes,' " she read aloud, " 'avail themselves of this building to transmit for future times the record of an awful event which occurred in this marketplace, hoping that such record may serve as a salutary warning against the danger of impiously invoking Divine Vengeance to conceal the devices of falsehood and deceit.' "

She paused, noting that both Vanessa and Catherine looked conscious. Of course the warning was more directed against blasphemy than against deception, but she doubted that they drew the distinction. She read on in a portentous voice.

" 'On Thursday 25th January, 1753, Ruth Pierce agreed with three other women to buy a sack of wheat, each paying due proportion; one of these women in collecting the money discovered a deficiency and demanded of Ruth Pierce the sum that was wanting; Ruth Pierce protested that she had paid her share and said she wished she might drop down dead if she had not. She rashly repeated this awful wish; when to the consternation and terror of the surrounding multitude she instantly fell down and expired.' "

The wording was less relevant than Sarah had hoped, yet her companions were a trifle pale. She managed to produce a realistic shudder and rubbed in the lesson. "What a shocking story! If I were guilty of any underhanded dealings, I vow I should quake in my shoes."

It was a silent pair that walked with her back to the Bear and allowed Peter to hand them into the barouche.

"What a pleasant day," sighed Sarah, leaning back against the squabs. "I fear Little Fittleton can be quite lonely now that all Adam's sisters are wed and removed from the neighbourhood. He means to bring his bride to live at Cheve, I collect, but how he will go on with such limited female companionship, I dread to think. Of course it is his growing up with so many sisters that is to blame."

"To blame?" asked Lady Catherine hesitantly.

"Yes. It is unconscionable the way he hides beneath such charm the lusts of a veritable Bluebeard."

"Bluebeard?" Vanessa's violet eyes nearly started from her head.

Catherine, however, looked slightly skeptical so Sarah hastened to retract.

"I exaggerate, of course. Why, I do not mean to accuse

dear Adam of murdering a series of wives! Indeed, I daresay he does not even mean to marry more than one at a time, though of course he does have radical views. Only the other day we were speaking of harems such as they have in Turkey, where a man is allowed four wives and any number of concubines—as many as he can afford to support, I believe, and Adam is excessively rich. Not that I have ever known him to support more than three females at a time, not counting his own family."

Vanessa gasped.

"My abigail did mention some such rumour among the servants at Cheve," Catherine conceded, her composure beginning to fray. "I dismissed it as an exaggeration."

"I fear not." Sarah sighed. "I was put in the uncomfortable position of receiving all three at the vicarage. At one time."

"Surely he will not expect his wife to receive his chères amies? Once I am Lady Cheverell, he will not continue to keep a mistress," Catherine stated confidently.

"You, Lady Cheverell?" cried Vanessa. "It is I who shall be his viscountess. He will have no cause to look elsewhere for beauty."

She and Catherine glared at each other. Sarah added her fuel to the flames. "Alas, Adam will never be satisfied with one woman, however beautiful or accomplished, whichever of you he chooses."

"He has already chosen me," said Catherine in a cold voice. "We have been betrothed since the day we went to Salisbury."

"Then I have prior claim," announced Vanessa in triumph, "for our engagement began on the night of the ball."

"On the contrary. Lord Cheverell clearly changed his mind after asking you."

"He is promised to both of you?" cried Sarah dramatically. "Alas, it is as I feared. Does he mean to keep one in London and one at Cheve, I wonder?"

Both young ladies stared at her, aghast. Unconsciously they moved closer together on the seat, as if for mutual protection. Sarah pressed her advantage.

"You will have to keep silent, of course. Think of the disgrace if it should become known, and I daresay even a peer can be imprisoned for bigamy. You will not like to be visiting him at Newgate."

Horror was mirrored in two pairs of eyes. Sarah sat back, satisfied.

"Lady Cheverell's house party comes to an end shortly, does it not?" she said in a conversational tone. "You will be glad to go home and tell your families that Adam has come up to scratch. Twice—though that is best kept secret. I wonder which of your papas he will approach first."

"If he has the audacity to ask my father for my hand," Lady Catherine announced, her voice steely, "I shall have him thrown out of the house."

"I shall write to Papa at once," Miss Brennan quavered, "and tell him on no account to grant Lord Cheverell permission to court me."

Sarah thoroughly enjoyed the rest of the drive home. When they reached the vicarage, Peter jumped down to help her from the carriage.

"Not a word to anyone!" she whispered to the groom, slipping a shilling into his hand.

"I knows how to hold me tongue, miss," he said with a grin, tipped his hat and drove on.

Adam looked up in annoyance as the door to his study was flung open. Not that going over the estate accounts was a pleasure, but having settled to them he wanted to finish and forget them. He had explicitly instructed Gossett that he was not to be disturbed.

The sight that met his eyes was not reassuring. Lady Catherine marched in, militant outrage personified. Vanessa Brennan, on the other hand, drooped, her beautiful violet eyes reproachful. Adam rose and bowed.

"To what do I owe the honour, ladies?" he enquired warily.

"Philanderer! Yes, you may well blench, my lord, for we know you to be a second Casanova!"

"Why, Lady Catherine, I am shocked that you have even heard of that notorious libertine."

"You need not think to cozen us with your wiles. All has been revealed to us."

"False deceiver, you have broken our hearts."

"What, both of them? Or have you more than one apiece?" Adam was beginning to enjoy himself. "What is this 'all' that you have discovered?"

"It is beneath our dignity to repeat the sordid details. Suffice it to say that you may consider yourself jilted, as you deserve. Twice. Come, dearest Vanessa, we will not bandy words with this—this—"

"Bluebeard," put in Miss Brennan helpfully as they swept out.

Accounts abandoned, Adam went after them, grinning. What the devil had Sarah told them?

"Gossett!" he shouted. "Have Caesar saddled and send Wrigley up to my chamber at once."

Not half an hour later he stepped into the vicarage study, to be greeted by two laughing faces. At the sight of him, both the Meades went off into fresh whoops. Jonathan's chair teetered precariously on two legs.

"Minx," said Adam, resigned. "What yarn did you spin to them?"

"I started quite innocuously," Sarah gasped, "with Lord Sidmouth's column."

The viscount looked blank.

"He is so rarely here he probably doesn't know about it," Jonathan advised his sister.

"You must remember the story of Ruth Pierce, who dropped dead in the market? It was dinned into us often enough when we were children as a dreadful warning against falsehood." Sarah explained how she had enticed the young ladies into reading the cautionary tale on the new market cross. "I am certain it gave them pause. However, Bluebeard was my trump card."

"Vanessa said something about Bluebeard. Sarah, you didn't tell them that I am in the habit of murdering my brides?"

"That was unnecessary. The truth was sufficient," she said dryly, then conceded, "though I cannot deny misleading them a little. I believe I succeeded in persuading them that you wanted two wives, one for the town and one for the country. What happened?"

"They invaded my study, arm in arm, insulted me, and informed me that I might consider myself jilted. Twice."

Once again Sarah and Jonathan howled with laughter. Adam joined in, but he was the first to grow sober.

"That's all very well, and I must thank you for your good offices, Sarah, but what about Lydia?"

"Miss Davis?" The vicar's chair landed on four legs with a thump. "What has she to do with this bumblebath?"

Surprised at his friend's frowning earnestness, Adam looked a question at Sarah.

"I did not tell Jonathan about Lydia." She seemed uneasy. "Her case is so very different."

Jonathan stood up, leaning on his desk with both hands, and fixed Adam with piercing grey eyes. "You cannot make me believe that Miss Davis trapped you into offering for her," he said, quiet but firm.

"I trapped myself." Adam shrugged, with a rueful smile, as the vicar relaxed somewhat and sat down again. "The poor child was desperately embarrassed and I sought only to calm her. Now your sister informs me that I cannot honourably cry off, and I am forced to agree with her."

"She is not a poor child, but a sensitive, compassionate and high-principled young woman. I am sorry that you are unaware of the prize you have won, but you will come to realize it in time. Sarah, I must ask you to promise me that you will not play off your tricks on Miss Davis. I will not have her hurt."

Again Adam glanced at Sarah, but she was preoccupied and seemed unaware of her brother's unexpected vehemence.

"I promise," she acquiesced. "Did I not say that her case is different? Do you . . . do you think the engagement should be announced at once?"

"Not yet." A tinge of pink coloured the vicar's cheekbones. "Not, at least, until Lady Catherine and Miss Brennan are gone. It can only humiliate them."

Adam agreed with alacrity, though it was a brief respite since his guests were to depart on Monday, some four days hence. He took his leave, and rode home puzzling over Jonathan's curious reaction.

Chapter Nineteen

<+- -+>

Sarah had just rolled out the gingerbread dough when Mr. Swanson and Lord James Kerridge appeared at the open back door of the kitchen.

"Come in, gentlemen." She wiped beads of perspiration from her forehead with the back of her wrist. "We are in for a thunderstorm, I think."

"Sultry weather," said Mr. Swanson, fanning his red face with his hat.

"Hot," agreed Lord James. The heat of the day and the greater heat of the kitchen had no discernible effect on his handsome countenance, but he looked apprehensive.

"Is Mrs. Hicks about?" enquired Mr. Swanson.

"She is upstairs, helping Nellie turn the beds." Sarah thought he, too, wore a slightly hunted air. "Did you wish to speak to her? I can call her down."

"No, no, I wouldn't disturb her for the world." He ran his finger round inside his collar. "The fact of the matter is, we wanted a private word with you, Miss Meade. Didn't we, Kerry?"

Lord James was eyeing the dough wistfully. He started, and said, "Private word, that's right. I say, Miss Meade, can I cut out some gingerbread men for you?"

"Do," she invited cordially, handing him a knife. "The children loved the shapes you came up with last time. What

178

was it you wanted to speak to me about, Mr. Swanson?"

"Kerry!"

His lordship started again and looked up from the very creditable pig he was carving from the dough. "You made me cut his tail off."

"Get on with it, man."

"Couldn't you go first?"

"Dash it, it was you who insisted on tossing for the right to go first."

Lord James looked as if he wanted to dispute this statement but he thought better of it and said pleadingly, "You say it for me, Swan. You're much better with words."

"The devil!" In the grip of strong emotion, Mr. Swanson forgot the deference due to a lady's ears. "I agreed to stay with you but I'm damned if I'll speak your piece. We're rivals, after all."

Much entertained, Sarah asked gently, "Did you have something to say to me, my lord?"

"Want to ask you to marry me," he blurted out. "Mean to say . . . Do me the honour . . . Offer my hand and heart . . . There, I told you, Swan, I've ruined it," he ended miserably.

"Not at all," Sarah assured him. "Your meaning is perfectly plain, and most flattering."

"Then you will?" There was as much alarm as gratification in his expression.

"Hey!" interrupted Mr. Swanson. "There's to be no pressing for an answer until I've had my turn. Miss Meade, though we have been acquainted so short a time, I have never met a woman I admired more. Pray allow me to express my fervent hope that you will do me the inestimable favour of accepting my hand and heart in marriage."

"Has a way with words, don't he?" said Lord James.

"Forgot to say, m'brother's a marquis. Ladies like that. I ain't exactly plump in the pocket but not run off my legs, neither. Stand the nonsense for a snug little house in town, pretty dresses and such. Course, Swan here was born hosed and shod. Daresay he could buy an abbey, though it beats me why anyone would want to do such a bacon-brained thing."

"If Miss Meade wants an abbey, I shall buy her one."

Sarah regarded the two anxious faces turned towards her. For a moment she was almost tempted. Lord James was good-looking, amiable, a member of the nobility. Mr. Swanson was clever, considerate, and rich enough to buy her everything she had ever coveted. Either of them would take her away from here, from the pain of seeing Adam with his chosen bride.

She sighed. It was impossible. Kerry was a dear fellow, but she thought of him as a younger brother, and her affection for Swan was for a kind friend and amusing companion. She shook her head.

"I'm sorry." She searched for words.

"No need to say another thing." Swan pressed her hand. "I daresay it wouldn't fadge. We can still be friends?"

Sarah blinked back an unexpected tear. "Of course. I hope we shall always be friends. Now, do you mean to help me cut out the gingerbread before the dough dries out? Kerry, pray make another pig. Johnny Cratch looks after his family's pigs and it will delight him. Swan, here's a knife for you. I leave it to your imagination. I must grease the baking tins."

From the merriment that ensued, she gathered that no hearts were broken. The gentlemen stayed to sample the gingerbread hot from the oven, then Mrs. Hicks came down and chased them out of her kitchen. A crack of thunder sent them in haste to their horses just as the first heavy drops of rain fell from the black sky.

Jonathan had gone to the next village on church business. Sarah hoped he would take shelter in a parishioner's house until the storm was over. On his return he would want to start writing his sermon, so she went into the study to make sure that ink and well-sharpened pens were awaiting him. Mrs. Hicks had closed all the windows, and the room was hot and airless. Beyond the French doors rain was falling in torrents by now and the clouds rumbled ceaselessly, but the wind was blowing from the opposite side of the house. Sarah opened the doors to let in a breath of coolness.

She stood there for a moment, enjoying the fresh air. The downpour was scattering rose petals and beating the Canterbury bells to the ground. Arthur would not be happy. She shrugged, and was turning away when a drenched figure dashed from the stables towards the kitchen door.

It looked as if Jonathan had sadly mistimed his return. Sarah hurried to the kitchen. It was Adam who stood there, dripping on the tiles, and raising a gingerbread shape to his mouth.

"We just brought in the last of the barley in time," he announced.

"Not the pig!" said Sarah. "That's for Johnny Cratch. Take Kerry's sailing ship—that's it, the one that looks like a thundercloud—and then for heaven's sake go up and change into something of Jonathan's before you catch your death."

"Yes'm." His lordship grinned and obeyed.

The vicar was taller but narrower in the shoulders. Fortunately, he by no means favoured the extremes of fashion, preferring to be able to breathe in his coats, so Adam eased into one without splitting the seams. He had a nervous moment with the pantaloons, but the knit fabric allowed some leeway. He rolled up the bottoms of the legs and the cuffs of the sleeves, slipped his feet into a pair of carpet slippers and went down with his own sodden clothes to the kitchen.

"Soon dry 'em out, my lord," promised Mrs. Hicks. "Miss Sarah's in the parlour."

Sarah giggled when she saw him. "Tea or Madeira?" she offered. "It must be all of ten years since you borrowed Jonathan's clothes. I see you are quite different shapes now. I'm surprised you can move."

"I'm not sure I dare sit down." He lowered himself carefully onto a straight chair. "Madeira, please. You're a fine one to laugh, my girl, with flour all over your forehead. Kerry was here making gingerbread, was he?"

"And Swan, too." She took out a handkerchief and brushed at her forehead without much success.

Adam desperately wanted to help her, to take her chin in his hand and . . . Cleaning the flour off her face was the last thing on his mind. He sat still.

She gave up the attempt and passed him his glass of wine. "I must look a shocking mess," she said. "That makes it even funnier."

"Do you mean to share the joke, or shall you sit there tantalizing me with your chuckles until I beg for mercy?"

"I ought not to tell you, but I know I can trust you to keep it to yourself. I received two proposals of marriage over the kitchen table."

Expecting to laugh, Adam was overtaken by unreasoning fury. "Which did you settle for?" he asked stiffly. "Good looks and a title and no brains, or wits and money and no looks?"

"Who am I to demand perfection? That was unkind,

Adam. They are your friends, or I should never have mentioned it. I am very fond of both of them, whatever their shortcomings."

"Fond!"

"In fact, I was tempted to accept them both, just to discover what is the attraction in being betrothed to several people at once, but it was a trifle awkward with both of them there."

Adam felt his cheeks grow warm but for the moment he ignored her deliberate provocation. "You mean they both proposed at once?"

"Heavens, no. They had tossed a coin, I collect, for the right to go first, and Kerry won. You can imagine that in such a predicament the poor fellow found himself tongue-tied even with me. He begged Swan to speak for him."

"And Swan obliged?" He was beginning to see the amusing side of the situation.

"He declined, on the grounds that they were rivals. Kerry stammered through a proposal, Swan followed with a polished bit of oratory, and Kerry congratulated him on his way with words. Whereupon I refused their kind offers and we finished making the gingerbread."

"A remarkable scene," he said, grinning. "I wonder you managed to keep your countenance."

"It was funny, but it would have been too shabby in me to have laughed. It was touching, too."

"Not to mention flattering! Of all my acquaintance I'd have wagered those two were the least likely to risk their heads in parson's mousetrap. And the more flattering when you had flour all over your face at the time."

Sarah's smile was wry. "I believe they, like you, felt that there was safety in numbers. I do not doubt their sincerity, but how could I accept one and refuse the other?"

183

"Did you want to accept one of them?" Adam hoped his dismay was not obvious.

"Oh no, both or neither. With your example before me, how could I be satisfied with less?"

"I assure you, the joys of being popular with the opposite sex are grossly exaggerated. In future I shall be faithful to one."

"I am glad, for Lydia deserves it."

Adam was in no position to explain that Miss Davis was not the female he meant to be faithful to, for he had no idea how to escape that entanglement. Then he recalled Jonathan's spirited defence of the girl, and her ease in the vicar's company. His usual optimism reasserted itself.

"Sarah, will you do me a favour? Lydia and I ought to be better acquainted before our engagement is announced, but if she stays on at Cheve, we might as well put a notice in the *Gazette*. Besides, Mama has a notion to go home with Louise to see her grandchildren. It is odd, incidentally, that she is so little downcast by the apparent failure of her plan to find me a bride! She keeps muttering that she knew my sisters would never find anyone suitable and she hopes my eyes have been opened. What do you suppose she means by that?"

"I've no idea. What is this favour you wish to ask of me?"

"You like Lydia, do you not? I am sure she considers you her friend. Will you invite her to stay here at the vicarage for a week or two?"

The bleak look that crossed her face almost made him retract his request. He chose instead to regard it as encouragement, for why should she look like that if she did not love him, despite his peccadilloes? What a fool he had been all these years!

"Very well," she said at last in a flat voice. "I shall write her a note at once and you can carry it with you when you leave. Help yourself to wine while I am gone."

Already hurrying towards the door, she did not see Adam's tender smile. He had a lowering feeling that there were tears in her eyes and he cursed himself for a brute, but he was determined to encourage an attachment between Jonathan and Lydia. It was the only glimmer of hope he had seen.

Chapter Twenty

Lydia Davis moved from Cheve House to the vicarage on Monday morning, when the rest of the guests departed. A groom sent to her parents had returned with their permission for her to prolong her absence.

"They are happy that I have made such amiable and respectable friends," she told Sarah.

"I confess I am slightly surprised that they do not object to your removing from a nobleman's mansion to a humble country vicarage. No doubt they are aware that you will continue to see Adam here. You did not tell them of your betrothal?"

"No, Lord Cheverell asked me to keep it secret a little longer. Do you not think a secret betrothal romantic? I daresay Mama and Papa guess that I will see him, but you must not think that they are excessively proud. Though they will be pleased if I marry a viscount, they both said before I left home that it is more important that I should be happy, as they are. What a charming room."

She was genuinely delighted with the tiny back bedchamber looking over the garden. It had been Sarah's as a child, and was decorated in faded chintz flower prints. A bowl of clove pinks on the dressing table scented the air.

"It is fortunate that you did not bring an abigail," said Sarah, "for I should not know where to put her."

"Lady Edward's dresser helped me at Cheve, and Mama's Darwin does at home, but I shall do very well without."

"My chamber is just across the landing there." Sarah pointed out the door. "You must call me if you need assistance with buttons and Nell will take care of your clothes. I hope you will enjoy your stay with us."

"I am looking forward to it. You will allow me to help you with your chores, will you not? And I should like to go with you on parish visits, if it will not disturb people. I always go with Mama to visit the tenants and the cottagers."

Sarah was surprised at this request, but she soon discovered that Lydia's ethereal romanticism hid a strong streak of practicality. She had been brought up with a thorough understanding of housekeeping and was willing to turn her hand to any task. What was more astonishing, the timidity so evident in her dealings with her equals vanished in the presence of her inferiors in station. Not that she treated them with condescension; on the contrary, she chatted happily with farmers' wives, sympathized sincerely with the aching bones of the elderly and, above all, adored the children.

"I need not be always on my guard against making mistakes," she explained when Sarah expressed her surprise. "Like you and Mr. Meade, they understand that I mean well and they will not look down their noses at me if I curtsy to the wrong person first or have a hole in my glove. When shall you open your school?"

"I have not thought of it in an age." Sarah found it difficult to summon up any interest. "If Jonathan takes the position in Salisbury, I cannot run a school here. It is better that I do not raise any hopes until I know whether it will be possible."

"In Salisbury!" Lydia looked aghast. "You are going to live in Salisbury? I did not know it. I thought when Lord Cheverell and I are married, you would always be close by."

"It is not settled yet. I daresay we might as well go and look at the church hall here to see what would be needed to turn it into a schoolroom."

The church hall was a plain flint-and-stone building used for harvest home suppers, Christmas assemblies and wedding breakfasts. Its windows were high under the eaves, its walls whitewashed and somewhat grubby. Lydia looked round and immediately began to plan new, colourful paint, pictures on the walls, desks and benches and a stove for cold days.

"You must talk to Adam about it," Sarah advised her.

"To Adam? I had thought Mr. Meade . . ."

"Adam has promised his support. Since he will be paying the bills, it is only right that he should be consulted."

"Yes, of course." Lydia's enthusiasm subsided.

Jonathan had accepted the news of their unexpected guest without protest, and at first had gone out of his way to make her feel at home. When Sarah described the girl's eager and practical involvement in household and parish duties, he pointed out that he always said they were underestimating Miss Davis. However, after the first few days he seemed to be avoiding her, spending more time than usual away from home and shutting himself in his study for hours at a time. He always joined the ladies for a while in the evenings, though, and they often sang together. Lydia's pure voice was a source of never-ending delight to both the Meades.

Sarah attributed her brother's preoccupation to the difficulty of deciding the future course of his life, for the acceptance or refusal of the cathedral position amounted to no less. Adam's absence was more puzzling. After escorting his betrothed to the vicarage he was not seen for a week, which was not, as Sarah told him when at last he did put in an appearance, the way to get to know her better.

"I am being tactful," he said.

"Tactful! I do not call it tactful to persuade me to invite her and then to vanish from the face of the earth!"

"Not from the face of the earth, only from this vicinity. Peggy's Billy returned last Saturday, did he not, for the reading of the banns? I prefer not to meet him before that knot is tied."

"Yes, he is back. Jonathan found him lodgings with one of the farmers. I must go and see Peggy again to make sure she has everything she needs for the wedding. In the circumstances, it must be a quiet affair, but you will attend, will you not?"

"Do you think I should? I own it will be a pleasure to witness that happy ending. Peggy is still living with the witch? Amazing."

"You cannot suppose she would be cowed by a sharp tongue after the adventures she has survived. Goody Newman dotes on her, as a matter of fact. Lydia and I called at the cottage last week and the old woman has never been better cared for."

"Lydia has not been a burden to you, I hope."

"She is the sweetest-natured creature, and most helpful besides. She will make you a good wife, Adam."

Despite this assurance, it was noticeable that Lydia reverted to her formal manners in Adam's presence, though she seemed less shy of him than before. He treated her like a delicate piece of valuable porcelain. Sarah saw this as a sign of his growing love, but she thought it quite the wrong approach. Lydia viewed Adam as a romantic and unapproachable hero, while he considered her to be fragile and helpless. Neither had the least notion of the other's real character.

While Sarah was still wondering whether it was her duty to try to rectify their distorted visions, or whether that would be unconscionable meddling, Adam departed again. Lord Lansdowne had invited him to Bowood for a few days, he said. It was an opportunity not to be missed.

Several days of rain intervened and it was not until two days before Peggy and Billy's wedding that Sarah and Lydia set off in the gig for Goody Newman's cottage. They had used the time to make the bride a couple of dresses for a wedding present. Peggy was delighted with the pretty sprigged muslins, and declared she would save them for Sunday best.

"Ye'd do better to stay put wi' me, my girl," muttered the old woman. "Men's no good, the lot on 'em. On'y one thing on their minds. What'll I do wi'out you?"

"I'll find someone else to take care of you," Sarah soothed her.

"One o' them useless village hussies, eh, miss? Or be there another o' his lordship's doxies willing to do for a pore ol' creetur? By all accounts, he c'd staff a mansion wi' his cast-off harlots. Reg'lar rakeshame, his lordship, fer all his winning ways."

"Now, Goody, don't you go talking like that afore the ladies," Peggy admonished.

It was too late. Lydia stared in horrified fascination at Peggy and asked, "You were Lord Cheverell's mistress?"

Peggy and Sarah exchanged a glance and Sarah shrugged her shoulders. Everything was known in the village and sooner or later the truth would out. It would be much worse for Lydia to hear about it after she was married.

"That I were, miss," Peggy confirmed, "and proud of it."

"What'd I say," grumbled Goody Newman. "All arter the same thing, men."

Sarah decided that was enough of the subject and she began to discuss the arrangements for the wedding. As soon as everything was settled, she and Lydia left. Lydia was looking rather dazed and had not opened her mouth since Peggy's revelation. As Dapple picked his way down the grassy track, Sarah braced herself for the questions she was sure would follow.

They had nearly reached the vicarage before Lydia turned to Sarah. "What did she mean about . . . about starting a mansion with . . ." Her voice trailed away.

"My dear, all young gentlemen have lady friends."

"Your brother does not!"

"Jonathan is a clergyman. The cases are different. Once you and Adam are wed . . ."

"Never! I will never marry a libertine," she cried passionately. "Oh, why did you not warn me, Sarah? Pray stop, I must talk to Mr. Meade."

Since they were about to turn into the drive, Sarah did not heed this request. Lydia jumped down from the slow-moving gig, stumbled, recovered herself, and ran into the vicarage, leaving the front door open.

Sarah drove round to the stables and left Dapple to Arthur's care. With dragging steps she moved towards the house. It was her duty to reassure Lydia, to reconcile her to Adam's past misdeeds, yet how could she do so when her heart had leaped with joy at those words of rejection?

Try as she might, she could not forget his brief kiss that misty day.

She paused outside the French doors to the study.

Within, her brother and Lydia were standing close together, talking earnestly. Jonathan was far better equipped to help the naive girl understand and forgive her betrothed, Sarah told herself, and she turned back to enter by the kitchen door.

"If anyone asks for me, I am gone walking," she told Mrs. Hicks as she passed through.

She went upstairs and changed into an old walking dress. The last clouds had blown over and the day was growing warm, so she put on sandals and her straw hat. She longed for the soothing peace of the open hills, the sense of perspective that only age-old Stonehenge could bring to her troubled spirit.

Slipping down the stairs, she saw that the study door was open. She should make sure Lydia was restored to tranquility before she sought her own solace.

Sighing, Sarah crossed the hall. There was a murmur of voices in the study.

As she reached the door, she heard Jonathan say firmly, "Quite sure."

"Then I am free again!" It was Adam. "Ever since Mama decided it was time for me to take a wife, I have felt prison walls closing in. That house party was a cockle-headed notion at best." His laugh was joyous, unconstrained.

It was too much for Sarah's fragile composure. She fled.

Returning to Cheve for Peggy's wedding, Adam had stopped at the vicarage on his way home. The front door was open, so he tethered his team and strolled in. Led to the study by the sound of voices, he had entered the room just in time to see his betrothed fling herself into the arms of his best friend.

"Ahem! I trust I do not interrupt?"

Two startled faces swung towards him. The vicar flushed

and released Lydia, but she clung to him.

"I love Jonathan," she told Adam defiantly.

"Betrayed!" He struck a dramatic attitude, clutching his chest. "Don't look so alarmed, Miss Davis, I am roasting you. To tell the truth, I suspected this might happen. Jonathan has been your fervent admirer for weeks, if I am not mistaken?"

"Was it so obvious? I had not intended to steal your bride, and I doubt her parents will thank me for it."

"No need for them to know we were ever betrothed."

"I do not care if you are not rich and titled, Jonathan. I shall like being a vicar's wife. I am sorry to disappoint Lord Cheverell, but I do not want to be married to him."

"You are quite certain?" Adam wanted no misunderstandings to bedevil him at a later date. When Jonathan answered for his beloved, "Quite sure," Adam laughed. "Then I am free again!" After some remarks on his mother's folly in thinking his sisters capable of finding him a wife, he went on to enquire, "Have you come to a decision about the cathedral post, Jonathan? I mean to try to bribe you to stay here. It is time the living was increased, and even with Sarah gone you will need a bigger house once your family begins to grow."

"Where is Sarah going?" asked Lydia in dismay. "I shall need her to show me how to go on."

"Not far. To Cheve, I hope."

Jonathan looked at him in astonishment. "You want to marry Sarah?"

"If she will have me."

"There can be no doubt of that. I never dreamed there was the least chance of your offering, and I warned her not to wear her heart on her sleeve."

"But I have done my best, these past few weeks, to destroy any regard she may have had for me. I have wasted years. Now I have come to my senses, I shall woo her and win her if it takes the rest of my life. Where is she?"

A short time later, Adam drove down the Amesbury road, praying he was right in guessing that Sarah was bound for Stonehenge. He did not pass her on the road, but on so fine a day she would have walked cross-country.

He paced among the towering stone arches, with growing impatience, for half an hour before he saw her limping towards him. He hurried to meet her.

"You have hurt yourself!"

"No, it's that dratted sandal strap the cobbler mended. It has just this minute broken again. What are you doing here?"

"I came to drive you home. I feel it is my duty to rescue you whenever your sandal strap breaks."

He swept her up in his arms, carried her to the altar stone, set her down and sat beside her. Close beside her.

"Adam?" She was breathless and confused, and adorably flushed.

"Will you marry me?"

"Adam! What of Lydia?"

"A momentary folly, now happily rectified, for I left her in your brother's embrace. They will make a match of it. Will you marry me?"

"Why?" she asked bluntly.

"Because I love you." He reached for her hand but she moved away.

"How many women have you said that to?"

"None, before you. Sarah, I have done many foolish things in my life, but none that I am ashamed of. You know all there is to know. Can you not forgive and forget?"

"The past is not mine to forgive. It is the future I am

thinking of." She raised her eyes to his, searchingly. "As your wife I could not bear your fickleness . . . because I love you."

He took her hands in his and would not let her withdraw, seeking words to reassure her. "You need not fear ghosts from the past. Janet is content with her husband, Marguerite has a new protector, Peggy will soon be wed to her Billy, and all my betrothals have ended with my being jilted. And you call *me* fickle! As for the future . . . Sarah, you will have to trust me. Is that too much to ask? I love you, and I would never willingly do anything to hurt you."

He let go one of her hands and ran his fingers through his hair. A single corn-gold lock fell back over his forehead. In all the years Sarah had known him that wayward curl had always been there, and suddenly the sight of it crystallized all her feelings for him. She raised the hand he had released and touched it with her fingertip, tenderly. He caught her hand, pressed it to his cheek.

"I trust you," she said. "I will marry you."

Adam gathered her into his arms, and the kiss he gave her then was no fleeting touch. At last she pulled away, breathless.

"I think I have always loved you." She leaned against him, gazing up into his blue eyes. "It has taken you an excessively long time to decide I am the one you want to marry."

"Not so long, if you consider that it is less than two months since first Mama persuaded me to think seriously of marriage. In fact I began struggling towards the correct conclusion immediately—you know the complications which arose. I knew that you were the only one for me as soon as you told me I must marry Lydia. Yes, you may laugh, but why do you think I sent her to stay with you and

Jonathan and then kept away?"

"I never guessed there was more than friendship between them. I never dared hope that you might one day feel more than friendship for me."

"A great deal more. After wasting so much time, I cannot wait three weeks to make you mine. Jonathan's bishop must give us a special license. Or did you want a splendid wedding, my darling?"

"A quiet one will be much more to my liking." Happy as she was in his arms, there was something she had to know. She reminded herself of Adam's oft-repeated dictum, that he could say anything to her. What was sauce for the goose, was sauce for the gander. She looked down, fixing her gaze on the daisies and willing herself not to blush. "Adam, Peggy said . . ."

"Sarah, let the past lie!"

Though he did not move, she felt his disappointed withdrawal and hurried on. "Listen, Adam, please. Peggy said that you are one of a very few men who . . . who try to please their *petites amies*. Then she said that even those few would be shocked to discover that their wives took pleasure in . . . in you know what."

His hand caressed her chin as he tilted her face towards his. "My dearest girl, I promise upon my honour that my wife shall learn to take pleasure in . . . you know what." His grin was wicked. "Now, so that I am not forsworn, you must come closer and I shall begin your lessons this very minute."

And he did.